FEELS ON WHEELS

.

TRACY BROEMMER

Feels on Wheels

by

Tracy Broemmer

Romantic Comedy

Published by Tracy Broemmer

Edited by Lexie Broemmer

Cover Images: Deposit Photos

Cover Design: Tracy Broemmer

All Rights Reserved

CHAPTER ONE

TWAIN

Jaws lopes out from the bend of woods on the back edge of the property with a bird flopping in his mouth again. Darn dog. I'd like to think he didn't grab that sucker alive, but I've seen him do it a time or two.

"Jaws." I stick my fingers in my mouth and whistle.

The German Shepherd mix trots a few steps and then puts it in high gear when he sees me.

"Whaddaya doin', bud?" I scratch his ears as he drops the dead bird at my feet. Jaws leans into my hand as I study the bird. Thankfully, this one looks like it's been dead awhile, so I can't blame my dog.

He decides he's had enough love and bounds back toward the woods, stopping on a dime when I whistle at him again.

"Home."

When I yell the word, Jaws drops his head like a little kid, pouting when his mom sends him home. I would know. I played my mom every chance I got when I was a kid. Still do, sometimes. Not my fault she hasn't caught on yet. Either that or she's got a soft spot for me.

I make sure my dog trots to the gravel drive at the side of the woods before starting the weed whacker again. Eyes on the ground, I trim the weeds around the rink's parking area, careful to keep the toes of my work boots out of range.

A car pulls into the lot behind me, and I hear four doors shutting and the excited chatter of little kids mixed with laughter from grown women. Pretty normal on this side of the property. Wolverine Park covers a hundred acres—some of them family friendly and some not. The skating rink, obviously, is for the kids. Plenty of adults go in; plenty of them end up sprawled on their butts with broken bones, too.

I lift my arm to rub the sweat off my face. I forgot I was still wearing the light flannel shirt I put on over my park t-shirt earlier. It was cooler at six in the morning. The late afternoon sun and the work on the grounds is making me warm. Ready to peel the shirt off, I prop the weed whacker on my leg and shrug it off my shoulders.

The noisy kids are racing each other across the gravel lot. I have a few nieces and nephews, and every one of them has crashed and burned there.

"Bryson!" One of the women calls. Both boys stop and turn to look, sliding a few inches on the gravel. Neither wipes out, but the woman tells them not to run. When the boys take off again, first at a fast walk and then, of course, at a run again, the other woman nudges the first with her elbow.

"Seriously? You think they're gonna listen?"

They're dressed in skinny jeans and those slip-on loafer sneakers that are all the rage right now. My sister has four pairs. Hair pulled up in nearly matching ponytails, the women look enough like twins that they have to be sisters.

Interesting. Maybe I should tell my brother we should dress alike. Truman would love that. The snort I make at the thought draws their attention to me.

"Hi." I nod and watch them walk by with their pale pink lips tipped up in smiles. If either of them wears makeup, it's light and natural. They say hi and keep going, one of them bumping into the mirror on the side of a car parked by the door—hard enough that she bounced off.

Ouch. Bet that hurt. I flinch and look away as I hear an ouch and a groan.

I see a lot of people around the family fun park. Most are friendly and talkative. We get a lot of locals, as the place has been here for over twelve years. It's changed a lot, hopefully for the better. Since I took the helm, we've grown the place into a major tourist attraction. Took some work. The zoning was right, but some locals fought us on the expansion and the update to the current attractions. Mostly, they're over that now. Parts of Wolverine Park are open year-round, so those tourist dollars are pretty steady all year long.

We keep it looking nice, too. I'm meticulous about the grounds and the buildings. The landscaping is always well-kept, paint's always fresh, and the interiors of the buildings are neat and inviting. It's not even so much that I want to keep the city officials from breathing down my neck. It's just who I am. My daddy taught me pride of ownership.

Granted, I got started on Daddy's dime, but I went to school, and I worked my butt off on several jobs during those years and after. I worked for Daddy, too, and I socked all that money away. I don't need much. I've got an old farmhouse at the back edge of the property where I live with Jaws—didn't pay for him. He's a stray that wandered down my drive a couple of years ago. I fed him and bathed him when he stuck around for a few days. No collar. No tags. No chip. He must have decided he liked me alright, because he stuck around.

Jaws and I drive an old Chevy pickup that's got some miles on it. Still runs. Perfect for me. My siblings are both high maintenance people; they take after our father. Apparently, the middle child—me—got my maternal grandfather's personality. My simple life leaves Truman and Harper baffled.

I put the weedwhacker back on the trailer and eye the land around the rink. Looks good. Most people are surprised I don't hire this stuff out. The groundskeeping alone here is a full-time job. But it's what I do. It's what I *want* to do. I check to make sure the tractor is secure on the trailer and then climb into the truck. I need to get this equipment put away and check one of the faucets in the girls' bathroom at the rink.

Mila Fuentes, my second-in-command, lifts her chin in my direction when I park the truck in front of the garage —also always well-kept and neat. I jump out of the truck and head back to the hitch.

"Pax is working on the a/c unit in number one." She bends back over the chassis of another trailer. Like me, Mila is a jack-of-all-trades. She peeks at me now, and I notice a steak of oil and dirt on her face. The difference being she cleans up and looks good in a dress. Then again, I've never tried one, so who knows what I'd look like in one.

"Good." I release the lock mechanisms and the safety pins and then go back to the cab of the truck to jockey it around enough to loosen the hitch. "I'm gonna go take care of that faucet Nadine called about earlier."

"What's for dinner?" Mila asks me.

"Mom's pot roast," I tell her, savoring both the thought of the dinner plate Mom left and Mila's jealous eye roll. "C'mon over. There's plenty." She knows this. Mom babies me way more than she babies Truman. Must be the middle child thing. Or maybe she just likes me better —that's what I tell Truman, anyway.

"Got a date," Mila answers.

"Oh yeah? That's cool." I jump back down from the truck and check the hitch again.

"Going to Charter's."

"Why would you go there when you know food and service is better right here at the Cabin?"

"You don't bring your dates around here."

With the hitch released, I go back to the cab of the truck, but I lean around my open door to look at Mila.

"I don't date."

CHAPTER TWO

MABRY

"Bryson!" My sister yells at her son again. He shoots her a little grin and shrugs his shoulders. He and his friend are so excited about going roller skating, they aren't listening to anything Barrie is telling them. They ran through the parking lot and just about wiped out. Then again, it was me who cracked my elbow on that car's mirror. The mirror's fine, but I'm still rubbing my arm as Barrie and I follow the boys inside.

I haven't been in a skating rink in years—probably at least twenty. Barrie and I used to go to skating parties when we were in grade school, but that's been a long time. Apparently, my ten-year-old niece went to a school skating party last month. But Bryson didn't get to go, because he had strep throat. Hence, Barrie and I are here to roller skate with Bryson and his friend Joel.

"Are you skating?" Barrie asks me as she forks out cash to pay our admission.

I snort and tip my head at her. "I haven't been on skates since I was Avery's age."

Barrie levels me with a look that says she's calling bullshit.

"Like that matters." She rolls her blue eyes at me. We look a lot alike, but lucky brat that she is, she got the blue eyes and I got gray. "You're a freakin' professional athlete."

"Nuh-uh," I argue.

"Close enough." She smooths two twenties out on the counter. Her nails are a bright, chirpy-looking pink. The perfect color to match her t-shirt. I don't do any shade of pink.

"Are *you* skating?" I look over her shoulder through the doorway to the actual rink. It's not crowded right now. On a late afternoon in June, I'm guessing most kids would rather be swimming. Bryson is finicky about getting water in his face, so he's not big on pools.

"Could be fun." She wags her eyebrows at me.

"I think the last time you said that was to Will, and now you have Bryson," I remind her.

She snickers. "Sort of true." She shrugs and continues, "I've said things to that extent many times since then."

Barrie and Will have been married twelve years. They've been together fourteen—started dating their senior year of high school, right before leaving to go to different colleges. Everyone told them it wouldn't last, but fourteen years later, my big sister's still happy and ridiculously in love.

"Do they serve alcohol at the concession stand?" I ask, but I'm kidding. A longneck might give me some courage, but since I haven't been on skates in years, probably not a good idea no matter that I am athletic. Not to mention, Barrie won't drink while we have Bryson and his friend here.

"Actually, I think they do."

"I'm kidding." I sigh and meet her eyes again. "Sure. Why not?"

She nods, notes the fact that I'm still rubbing my arm where I hit it on that mirror. I slip by her while she finishes at the counter and go on into the rink. Bryson and Joel are parked in front of an arcade game.

"Aunt Mabry, can we—"

I cut Bryson off with a quick shake of my head. Barrie would have a fit if she brought the boys here to roller skate only to have Bryson ask for money to play games. He and Avery have an Xbox, but Barrie and Will limit their time on video games.

"Are you kidding?" I drop my hands to their shoulders

and steer them to the skate rental counter. "We are here to roller skate, boys."

"Are you skating, Aunt Mabry?"

Barrie might have been lucky to find her true love so young. I've dated some fun guys, some nice guys, and my share of bad guys. And by bad, I don't mean sexy and intriguing. I mean laid off and not too concerned about it, rude and arrogant, and just not my type at all. The only guy I love with my whole heart and soul—well, other than my dad—is Bryson Holmes.

He squints up at me now waiting for my answer. His friend is dancing beside me. I'm thinking it's the gotta-pee dance little kids do. When Joel grabs his crotch, I wince and look for Barrie.

"I am, Bryson Holmes." I wink at my nephew as Barrie joins us. "Sizes? Joel needs the bathroom."

"Mmm." Barrie holds out her hand and Joel takes it without hesitation. She wanted more kids. If she had her way, she would have ten by now. As it happened, she had a hard time with both pregnancies, and her doctor advised her against another. I, on the other hand, have no idea what that experience would be like. Haven't tried to get pregnant. Haven't carried a baby. Haven't done things to make babies in a long time, come to think of it.

Do I want kids? Yes. As many as Barrie would have liked? No. I told her once when she was pregnant with Bryson, I could pump a few out and sell them to her. There might have been tequila involved.

Barrie tells me sizes to start with for the boys and takes them to the bathroom—Bryson grumbling that he doesn't have to go. The guy at the rental counter looks high. He's kind of cute but in a friend's-little-brother sort of way. He keeps swinging his head back to flip his kinky blond hair off his face. He's tatted up like a biker, but I'd bet my right arm he's not.

"Hey Cliffie." A guy appears behind him and claps him on the shoulders. "How's it goin' man?"

"Good." Cliffie nods and looks over his shoulder to smile at the guy. "Nadine taped that faucet off."

"I'll look at it," the new guy says with a nod. He moves around behind the rental counter like he knows it by heart. Tall and lanky, his moves are surprisingly fluid. He pulls a clipboard off a nail on the back wall, reads something, and then hangs it up again. "How ya doing?" He's looking at me now.

"Good. At the moment."

The guy smiles and reveals perfect teeth—the first thing I notice on a guy. Not that I'm checking him out. He leans in and rests his elbows on the counter and devours me with his twinkling brown eyes.

"We'll see how it goes out there." I nod my head at the rink.

"Good luck." He knocks his fist on the counter and then straightens to walk away. When Cliffie turns to select our skates, I take advantage of the chance to watch the other guy walk out the other end of the counter. Worn denim. A loose-fitting black t-shirt that says Wolverine Park on the front chest. Big cartoon wolverine on the back. It hits me that he's the guy who was using the weed whacker when Barrie and I were in the parking lot.

Pretty cute.

If I were in the market for a guy.

For now I'm going to rope Bryson up and get these skates on him and make him skate with me.

CHAPTER THREE

Twain

"Anybody in here?" I tap on the main door of the ladies' restroom, but I don't need to. I hear voices—a woman's and kids'.

"Bry, let's go."

There's an exchange between the kids—something about Optimus Prime, and then there's a noise like a jet fighter flying or more accurately, the noise a kid makes to sound like a jet fighter. The boys hurry out past me without even seeing me. The woman who follows gives me an apologetic smile.

She looks a lot like the woman at the counter. The one who plans to skate. Same colored ponytail. Same high cheekbones. But her eyes are different. Blue. The other woman's were gray. Both are pretty, but something about the woman at the counter sticks with me as I nod.

"It's empty now," she says.

"Thank you.

I slip past her and eye the dark, blue-tiled walls and floor. It's clean, as I expect. The garbage can isn't overflowing, which is something I stay on my employees about all the time. Nobody's pay grade is above keeping the park spic and span, least of all mine.

I peel the caution tape off the sink and throw it away. Nadine tends to go overboard. If no water comes out when you try the faucet, it's pretty obvious something's not working. I didn't bring the whole caddy of tools with me, but I do have a flathead screwdriver in my pocket. I use it to ply the handle cap off the center of the faucet. I need a Phillips head to tighten the screw. Hopefully that's the problem. Seems likely since the other faucets are working.

The women and the boys are on a bench changing into skates when I go back out to the rental counter. The boys are still discussing Optimus Prime in voices loud enough to earn them constant shushing. I wonder if they're brothers. Truman and I got along fairly well when we were kids, but we had our fights. Cliffie is tightening the wheels on a pair of speed skates when I join him behind the counter.

"I need a Phillips head," I tell him. He's holding one, but he reaches under the counter and pulls a Rubbermaid organizer tray out. "What is this?" I ask as I rummage through the tray. I grab the only Phillips I see and look at up at him.

"Pharrell Williams," he answers immediately. "You've heard it."

I stand for a second, eyes on Cliffie, as I listen to the song blaring over the speakers out there on the rink. I do recognize it, but it's not one I listen to often. I'm more of a country music guy. Oddly enough, you don't find a lot of kids who want to roller skate to country music.

"How's foreign policy class?"

Cliffie shoots me a grin and shrugs.

"Okay."

"Good."

I have an equal number of full time and part time employees. Some of my part-timers are retired folks who work for me for a little income and some fun. Others, like Cliffie, are students. Last week he was cramming for an American Foreign Policy Exam. Nice way to kick off the summer— taking a class like that at the local university. I don't miss my college days at all. Not even the partying. Yeah, it was good while I was there, but I'm over it. Harper and Truman call me an old soul. I guess there's some truth to that.

The problem with the faucet is fixed when I tighten up the screw. Relieved it's not serious, I return the Phillips to the tray under the counter and then mosey over to the concession stand to check things there. I don't have to be here. I've got people. My family is good-natured about reminding me of that. I could sit in the Woolff corporate office with them. I could find other work, they tell me. I could—I'm a hard worker, and I'm smart and social—but I like being out here on the campus all the time. My degree is in business management, but I would rather be actively involved in the physical labor around here than being stuck behind a desk here or elsewhere.

It's a Tuesday, so the rink isn't packed. There might be thirty people on the rink itself. Another fifteen in the concession area—kids and adults alike. I wave at familiar faces and stop at the counter to talk to Kelsea—another part timer. Unlike Cliffie, she's not a student. She's a single parent holding down two jobs and doing computer graphics stuff on the side just to make ends meet.

"Busy?" I ask her.

She screws up her baby face to think and finally shakes her head. "Not bad. But not like last night."

There's a theater here on the grounds. A five-star restaurant. A casino and nightclub. Go-kart racing and a little climbing wall for kids. Different times of the year are busy for each venue. Different nights too. But the casino is always packed; everybody's looking to hit the jackpot.

I drum my fingers on her counter as the music changes. This song is an oldie, one my parents skated to when they were kids.

"'Funkytown,'" Kelsea says with wonder in her voice. "Doesn't that mean sex?"

I snort and roll my eyes. Kelsea's not even twenty. The things that come out of her mouth amuse me to no end.

"Um." I shrug and turn my back to her, so I can see the rink. Disco lights flash everywhere, making the place feel cool and fun. The rink started as my parents' baby. Dad started investing in real estate when he was young. This is one of the first businesses he bought. He'd watched my granddad in the real estate market for years, so he knew what he was doing. Both of them have an uncanny sense for good investments. Come to think of it, so do Harper and Truman. I might, but I don't care to do more than running the family amusement park. I'm not into boardrooms, attorneys, and acquisitions.

Mom used to skate here every weekend with her girlfriends. My dad and his buddies came in one Friday night after tipping a few. That's how Dad says it. Looking for trouble. Dad says he found it when he laid eyes on Mom. He paid the rental for skates and made a fool of himself on the floor. But he got her attention.

While I'm standing here, I see the women and boys go out on the floor. The boys' skating is jerky and uncoordinated, picking their feet up and trying to get traction to go. The woman I assume is the mom holds their hands. The other one reaches for one of the boy's hands, but she hesitates when the kid says something to her.

She nods, and even from this distance, her smile lights the rink up brighter than the lights on the disco ball. She says something to the other woman, and they laugh, and then she skates off. She picks up speed, the smile on her face carefree like a child's. I move toward the rail as she nears the turn, worried that this is where she's going to crash. I'm a good skater—with my parents meeting here, all of us kids grew up on skates. That doesn't mean I haven't crashed, and those falls get worse as you get older.

She navigates the turn with ease and picks up speed again up the other side of the rink. Impressive. She looks like a natural. Nothing about her looks familiar; she's not even a sometimes visitor, let alone a regular. Her long legs eat up the floor, though she looks like she's dancing on skates, rather than trying to speed. Her hips sway with the beat of the new song. I know "Uptown Funk." Part of me feels kind of bad for standing here watching her, but it's not even that I'm checking her out. Well, it's not *all about that*, I guess. It's just fun to watch someone move so comfortably, with that kind of confidence.

I turn back to Kelsea and wave.

"Need me, call me," I tell her. She nods, and I go on and slip out the back door.

I could go on home, but I want to go check the casino first. I end my night with that final check-in there every evening. There's never much trouble, but it makes me feel better. My parents were a bit concerned when I decided to build it four years ago, but like the rest of the locals here, they're pleased with its success.

Mila eases her truck up the road on her way out for the night and slows when she nears me. She puts her window down and puts the truck in park.

"Loose screw."

She grins. "Rude."

"Enjoy your date," I tell her. "Even if you aren't coming here."

"I heard Becca's back in town."

"Don't care." I pat her door with my hand and step back.

"See ya, Twain."

CHAPTER FOUR

MABRY

I wasn't sold on the idea of roller skating when Barrie asked me to tag along. But this has been a blast. I missed so much of my niece's younger years, and I regret that. She's only ten, and I see her often enough that she knows who I am. But I hate that I never watched Barrie put skates on her and take her by the hand to lead her to the rink. Bryson and Joel were hilarious—all rough edges and stompy skates, losing their balance and crashing to the floor. I guess the good thing is that they're little enough, they don't have far to fall. That and young enough that they'll heal quicker if they do get hurt.

They kind of got the hang of it before we left, though they were hard core lean-hard-on-one-leg and don't-get-cute-with-it skaters. Still, even though Barrie did a bit of a crash stop on the rail and both Bryson and Joel fell a few times, no one got hurt. We stopped for a break—Barrie and I shared some nachos. And the boys had cotton candy. Barrie and I got to catch up a bit; I've only been back in Bassett for a couple of weeks, and I'm still settling in. So, catching up with my sister while the boys whispered and giggled and yelled in the concession area was fun, too.

"Avery wants to have her birthday party here," Barrie tells me as we follow the boys outside.

"That sounds fun." I nod.

"You know what would be really fun?" Barrie grabs my arm. The evening sun hangs low in the sky, but it's eye level, and I'm blinded after being in the rink for a couple of hours. The same truck from when we came in earlier is parked just outside the gravel lot. There's a guy walking toward it with his phone pressed to his ear—kind of looks like the guy from earlier, the one talking to Cliffie at the rental counter. He was kind of cute. Maybe if Avery has her birthday party here, I'll get to see him again.

"What?" I turn to look at Barrie as I step off the sidewalk into the gravel lot. Bryson yelps and jumps backwards knocking into me. My ankle twists, and the next thing I know I'm on the ground looking up at Barrie.

And she's laughing. Hysterically.

Bryson leans over me now and covers his mouth with his hands. I don't know where Joel went, and I don't have time to worry about it. I hear the crunch of work boots on gravel and squeeze my eyes closed.

"Hey!" A male voice. One that sounds a lot like the guy from earlier, talking to Cliffie at the counter. "Are you okay, ma'am?"

Ma'am? Did he really call me ma'am?

Barrie snorts and titters and wipes her eyes.

"I'm fine."

I have no idea if I'm fine. I haven't tried to move. I'm mortified to be spilled all over the gravel with a little kid standing over me with big eyes, looking at me like I'm an alien who fell from the sky and a woman giggling so hard over me that she's wiping her eyes.

"Hang on."

I turn my head to the left as those work boots stop by my side. The guy squats down and reaches out to touch my shoulder.

"Can you move?"

"I don't know yet," I tell him. "I'm too busy shooting death glares at my sister."

The guy grins, and his whole face crinkles up and swallows his warm brown eyes. From my angle, I see how long and thick his eyelashes are. Totally unfair for a guy to have lashes like that.

"That one right there?" He looks from me to Barrie who is now trying desperately to get herself under control.

"The one and only, thankfully. I'm not sure I could handle two of her."

The guy turns his attention back to me, his hand still light on my shoulder.

"Did you bump your head?"

"I don't think so."

"What happened?" Barrie asks. She finally sounds normal, but when I look up to meet her eyes, a little giggle shoots out of her mouth before she can stop it. "You were looking me in the eye one minute, and the next you were on your butt."

"Hinie, Mom," Bryson corrects her.

"Bryson tackled me."

"I saw a lizard," he mumbles with a shrug.

"A lizard?" I squeal. The guy wants to hold me down, probably to make sure I'm not injured and don't plan to sue the entertainment complex. But I don't do lizards. "Let me up. I'm fine. I'm fine."

Rather than keep me pinned, the guy moves with me, hunched over, one hand reaching to take mine and the other on my opposite shoulder as I climb to my feet. I might find some bruises later, but at the moment, the only thing hurt is my pride.

"Are you okay?" he asks again. "Do you need some ice?"

"I'm fine," I assure him.

"I take it you don't like lizards?"

"I—no. No, I don't like lizards."

"How about dogs?"

In the middle of brushing myself off, I look up at the guy with a frown.

"What?"

"Fair question. Do you like dogs?"

"Yes." I raise my brows, wondering if there's more to the question.

"Good. Because Jaws is worried about you." He nods his head at something behind me. Slowly, I straighten and look over my shoulder. A very serious-looking German Shepherd sits about a foot behind me, ears perked and ready, his aquamarine eyes glued to me.

Jaws? Did he say Jaws?

"Jaws?" I repeat and glance back at the guy. "His name is Jaws?"

From the corner of my eye, I see the dog flinch when he hears his name.

"Yep."

"Is he mean?" I whisper the words. "Will he attack me?"

"He's a dope," the guy answers. "He wouldn't hurt a fly."

I take a deep breath, relieved Jaws isn't a guard dog waiting to attack me for being a klutz on their property.

"Except for the birds he brings to me from down by the creek."

"Birds?"

"C'mere, Jaws." The guy holds his hand out, and the dog trots over to him with his ears tucked back to his head. He does look kind of dopey with his ears like that, and his eyes shut in appreciation as the guy scratches his head.

"What would be fun?" I ask.

"Anything here," the guy answers me.

"Barrie." I spin around to look for my sister. "What would be fun?"

Barrie wiggles her eyebrows at me, but when the guy glances at her, she turns it off and gives me a nonchalant shrug.

"Oh. I was just thinking you should have your birthday party here." She unzips her purse now to dig through it and look for her keys.

"Me." I narrow my eyes at her. "I should have my birthday party here?"

"That's a great idea," the guy agrees. By now, he's let go of my hand, and his other hand isn't on my shoulder. The embarrassed part of me is relieved, because I'm not an invalid, and I'm usually very surefooted. Not one to walk into side mirrors on cars or crash in gravel parking lots.

"Why would I have a skating party for my birthday?" I tip my head at Barrie.

"I just think it would be fun," she answers. "I'd love to have my girlfriends here to celebrate. Some good music, some skating, some drinks."

"Then maybe you should have your party here," I tell her. The guy tucks his hands in his pockets now and watches us. Jaws leans into him, as if trying to tell him he needs another head scratch.

"My birthday was last week," Barrie reminds me, as if I didn't grow up in the same house she did.

"Actually, you could do the whole scene. Skating. Go-karts. The casino." The guy shrugs. "We even have a couple of little bungalows we rent here for overnight stays."

Okay, so, that does sound fun. Still, I'm ready to get out of here right now. My butt does hurt a little. And I scraped my elbow when I went down. Nothing I won't survive, but the little sting and the ache in my backside is just a reminder that I just spilled all over the lot, and this guy—of all people—had to see me and come to my rescue.

"Mom, look at this."

Bryson holds his hand out to Barrie and then swings it around to me. Afraid he's befriended the lizard that started this whole mess, I dodge him and move to my left. And bump into the guy. Jaws warns me off with a low growl.

"It's a rock, Aunt Mabry." Bryson rolls his eyes.

"Bryson, dude!" Joel calls from down the front sidewalk. I glance at him, relieved he hasn't been playing in the middle of the parking lot. But when I see that he's holding a small garter snake, I jump again. Jaws barks a warning this time. I'm encroaching on his master, and he obviously doesn't approve.

"Mabry?" The guy grins when I look at him. "Mabry you tripped over that extra letter in your name. And that's why you fell."

I want to be irritated with him. After all, I lived through junior high and heard more than my fair share of teasing about my name. Doesn't help that my last name is Aliston. Two extra letters. Several boys in my seventh-grade reading class asked if my parents knew how to spell. The first day we played three-on-three in PE, I shut them all up. Maybe my parents can't spell or maybe they have an affinity for different names. But they gave me height and a little finesse and a gorgeous jump shot.

The grin on this guy's face is so charming I can't muster an ounce of irritation.

"Heard it before, Cowboy," I say with a soft laugh.

"Twain," he says.

I stare at him in silence for a second, probably looking confused, like the daughter of someone who can't spell *Maybe*. Does he think he's quoting Mark Twain? *Is he?* I was a decent student, but I wasn't the most conscientious, and I didn't always keep up on my reading. Then again, I'm ninety-nine percent certain Mark Twain didn't write about anyone named Mabry or anyone prone to accidents.

"What?" I finally shake my head and shrug. Behind him, Barrie and the boys are crossing the lot now. I see her brake lights blink when she aims the key fob at her Camry. Great. Barrie has decided I should flirt with this guy, so she's left me alone with him so I can bat my eyelashes and he can ask me out.

I'm not looking forward to Barrie's teasing, but I don't hate the idea of this guy asking me out.

"My name's Twain."

"Oh."

His grin turns sheepish as he dips his head. "My parents are big readers," he explains. "You should definitely have your birthday party here, Mabry."

"Maybe."

The word is out of my mouth before I know I'm going to speak. Because suddenly, I like the idea of having a skating party for my thirtieth birthday party. Never mind the possibility of broken bones. If it means running into Twain again, it might be worth the pain.

CHAPTER FIVE

"You're always working."

I look up at my sister as she steps onto the deck behind my house. I'm squatting to inspect the wood, wondering if it's time to bite the bullet and do vinyl. I stained the deck a couple of years ago, but it looks like it needs it again.

"I'm not working," I tell Harper as she moseys over to the patio table I splurged on last year. Becca would say I did it out of spite. That I waited until she left to do even one thing she asked me to do. But that's not true. For one thing, if Becca had picked the patio furniture, she would have found something ten times as expensive as what I bought. And it would be on the patio or deck of a McMansion in the Greystone Gated Community by the Basset Country Club, rather than the old farmhouse I live in.

The other thing—I haven't given much thought at all to Becca since the day she stormed out eighteen months ago, angry with me for not wearing a suit and tie to her friend's wedding reception. That was the straw that broke the camel's back for her, but in retrospect, it was the biggest issue between us ridiculously oversimplified.

Becca wants a glamorous life. I don't.

Harper sits down at the table and leans in to study the firepit in the center.

"What're you doing?" I join her at the table.

"Why don't you have this on?"

"Maybe because it's not cold?"

"It's sexy." She shrugs.

"Yeah? You think I'm out here on my deck gettin' sexy with myself?"

Harper snorts and rolls her eyes.

"Eww." She shakes her head and flops back to relax in her chair. "How's business?"

"Good."

It's the same answer I give anyone in my family who asks. Naturally, they all want more details.

"Twain."

"Casino's raking it in," I tell her. "Alcohol sales alone were up quite a bit last weekend. Now that it's spring and warm, the go-karts and batting cages are gonna start pulling more people in."

"Andy Garza's looking for a chief operating officer," Harper tells me. I know even without the pointed look she's giving me, she means I should be interested in the position. I'm not.

"Are you looking for a new job?" I ignore her look. "Because I'm not."

Harper laughs and slinks lower in her chair.

"You're allergic to office work, aren't you?"

"Why would I want to sit behind a desk when I can be outside in this all day?" I toss my hands up and look around my backyard. My house butts up against another stretch of the same woods up closer to the attractions, but I keep my yard immaculate. The grass looks like plush green carpet. My landscaping is top notch. Becca actually liked the landscaping here. Just not the house.

"Agree to disagree," she says the words she and I have adopted to end these discussions.

"Where's your crew?" I ask her.

"Sshh." She closes her eyes. "I'm hiding from them."

Harper is the oldest in the family, though she's only older than me by three years. She got married a few years after college and then popped three kids out, all while holding down her job as Dad's chief operating officer. Her kids follow our birth order—the oldest is a girl and the next two are boys. All of them are under ten. She hides out on my deck or in my house often.

"Kids need their mom, Harper."

She slits one eye open to stare at me.

"They're with Keith," she answers. "They need daddy time, too."

"Want a beer?"

"You know I do," she answers when I climb to my feet. I step inside the kitchen and grab two longnecks from the refrigerator. Jaws is parked at Harper's side when I go back out. Eyes still closed, my sister scratches his head and tells him he's a good boy.

She opens her eyes when I nudge her arm with the bottle.

"What were you doing?" She twists off the cap. "When I got here?"

"Trying to decide if I'm going to stain the deck again or replace it with vinyl."

"That's work."

"It's for my house." I roll my eyes.

"Becca's back in town."

There's no love lost between my sister and my ex. Harper never butted in during the two years Becca and I were together, but she made it obvious to me she didn't like her. Likewise, Becca never went for my family, because she knew family will always be more important to me than money. But she never cared to spend time with them, either.

"So I heard." I take a long pull from my beer and then rest the bottle on my knee.

"Who told you?"

"Mila."

"I love Mila," Harper says with a grin. From day one, Harper has tried to set me up with my right-hand woman. While I think Mila's attractive and fun, I have no intentions of dating her and screwing up a good friendship and work relationship. Not to mention I don't need my sister playing matchmaker.

"She had a date this week."

"Good for her." Harper nods as if to signal she's on Team Mila. "You're not gonna see Becca, are you?"

"Nope."

"There's gotta be a reason that gold digger's back in town."

"Maybe because her family lives in Bassett."

"Maybe because she can't find a guy half as great as you are, and she's back to get her hooks in you again."

All the maybes make me think of the woman who was here earlier in the week with her sister and the two little boys. *Mabry.*

Now, her I wouldn't mind bumping into again. If I were a kid, I might even cross my fingers that she ends up having a birthday party out here. That would be fun, I agree with her sister. And I wouldn't even be *at* her party. But I could figure out some way to see her and talk to her again if I knew she was here.

"Probably," I tell Harper with a lazy shrug. "I can't help that women want me."

Harper's laugh is loud and hearty. She flinches when we hear a car pull up out front, quickly followed by the slap of the screen door on my front porch.

"Mo-om!" Her oldest yells through the house. "Ethan wrote on the seat in the car!"

"They found you," I whisper as my niece bursts through the door onto the deck. Harper gives me the evil eye as Hattie bounces closer to her. She squats beside Jaws to pet him, but she keeps her eyes on Harper.

"He drew a smiley face on Dad's backseat," Hattie continues.

"Sounds like Dad's problem," Harper answers.

"Dad told him to wait until he talked to you."

Harper looks at me and rolls her eyes. Seconds later, we hear Harper's husband and the two boys in the kitchen. Ethan barrels out of the house and launches himself into my lap.

"What's for dinner?" My brother-in-law asks Harper as he steps outside.

"Whatever you're fixing," she answers without looking at him.

"Dad was going to get us pizza," my other nephew, Craig, tells Harper. He narrows his eyes at Ethan. "And then Ethan drew on the seat in the car, so Dad says we can only go if you say we can."

"We can't," Harper says simply.

"But Mo-om!" Hattie argues.

"Nope. Ethan, you're old enough to know better."

He probably is; five-year-olds should know better than to write on stuff, right? Ethan leans back into me.

"I'm staying with Uncle Twain."

"Can he, Mom?" Hattie jumps on that. "And then we can go get pizza."

Harper starts to argue, to say no. But as she stands, I cut her off. "He can stay. It's fine."

"Are you sure?" Harper sounds calm, but when she looks at me, I see the hopeful gleam in her eyes. She's an awesome mom, but I know she gets tired. And I love the kids, so I don't mind helping her out now and then.

"Yep." I nod and sling my arm around Ethan. "I'm gonna make this dude work, though."

"I wanna whack the weeds!"

"Did that earlier this week." I shake my head. "I need to clean my house. Your mom says you're pretty handy with the vacuum cleaner."

"Why don't you just get married so your wife can do that?" Craig asks me.

"Oh boy." I grit my teeth as both Hattie and Harper swing around to give him hell.

"You think Becca would have cleaned the house for Uncle Twain?" Hattie asks her brother.

Not the point Harper is going to make. My sister is a very powerful woman, formidable in business and pretty in charge of her whole family. Her husband included. She loves him; she loves her kids, but she's not going to take that comment lying down.

"Is that why you think Dad married me?" she asks Craig. "So I would clean his house?"

The eight-year-old, finally catching on to the fact that he might have said something wrong, looks around at all of us and then looks back at Harper with a big gulp.

"Can we go now? I'm hungry."

"Ethan, be good." Harper crosses to me and leans over to kiss her youngest goodbye.

"I'm always good," he says quietly.

"Right." Hattie rolls her eyes. "That's why you don't get pizza."

"But I want pizza," he argues.

Familiar with the scene, I smile at Harper and wave her away. Once they go inside, and me an Ethan are alone on the deck, I finish my beer and then set Ethan off my lap.

"Wanna grill some hotdogs?" I ask him.

"Do I getta manda grill?"

I chuckle as we go inside to get out the hotdogs.

"No way, man. I told you. You gotta be a big boy to man the grill."

"When will I be a big boy?"

"Why'd you write on Dad's seat?" I lift him to sit on the counter as I find hotdogs and some chips we can eat with them.

"Craig dared me to."

"Mmm." I nod. There may have been times I dared my little brother to do things just to get him in trouble. "Next time he dares you to do something, you should probably say no."

"Can Jaws have a hotdog, too?"

"No."

"Will you take me for a ride on the tractor?" Ethan tips head and gives me that sweet smile that melts my heart.

"Yes. After we eat, we'll take a ride."

"Grampa said the *f* word yesterday night."

With my back to Ethan, I laugh.

"Grama said he's bad."

I'm sure she did. My mom used to cuss like a sailor, same as my dad. She was hardcore and business-before-fun right up until the day Hattie was born. Then she shed that corporate skin and became a fun, protective grandma. She loves Harper's kids and Truman's little boy to bits and pieces. I just hope one day I can give her a couple of grandchildren, too.

CHAPTER SIX

MABRY

I played basketball at a Division 1 college. Loved it, but I never thought I had the stuff to go pro. My sister loves to tease me about it. Barrie's a good athlete, too, but she picked Will when she was so young, she didn't have the same range of opportunities I did. I studied speech and language when I was in school and took a position at a hospital as a speech-language pathologist when I graduated.

My grandmother got sick last fall, so without discussing it with my family, I started looking for positions in Basset, Illinois so I could move back home. I might have given up a cool second-story apartment in the city and great options for eating out and live music, but I'm excited about my move. I'm working in a hospital setting again, so even the job is familiar and comfortable.

I'm renting a house in a cozy little neighborhood about four blocks from my sister and her family. My parents are a ten-minute walk from me, if that. I'm happy being closer to my family, and I'm grateful that my grandmother is fighting the cancer and doing well.

Barrie and I have been spending a lot of time together, and on nights when she goes to a yoga class with her friends, I watch Avery and Bryson. She tried to talk me into doing the class with her, but I'm not big on yoga. I take a daily ride on my bike for exercise, and I want Barrie to have something that's hers. She has girlfriends in that class, and though I like her friends and don't mind tagging along, I respect her space.

Besides, I love having Avery and Bryson to myself for an evening every week.

"Will's out of town," Barrie tells me. She's standing by the door like she's suddenly afraid to leave her kids with me.

"Okay," I mumble absently. "Aves, let's make chicken burritos."

"Yes!" Avery jumps up from her spot on my couch and hurries into the kitchen.

"I just want cheese," Bryson hollers from his spot on the opposite end of the couch.

"Baby," Avery mutters in disgust.

"Avery—"

"Barrie." I finally look up from the video game Bryson shoved at me when they came in and meet my sister's eyes. "We're fine."

"Okay. I just..." She shrugs.

"Everything okay?"

Avery's busy digging things out in my kitchen, and Bryson is reading a picture book from the library, so I cross the living room to stand by Barrie.

"Yeah."

Not convinced, I study her face for a long moment.

"What?"

"You're not okay."

"Will and I got into it this morning."

"Oh."

News to me. Actually, it's almost a relief to know they fight. I've never seen it happen.

"Bryson said you guys played games all night last week."

I draw back, kind of feeling like Barrie sucker punched me.

"We played Chutes and Ladders." I fold my arms over my chest and cock my head, ready to defend my case. "We played Monopoly. Bry was my partner. We played Hangman. And Scrabble."

"Bryson said you played video games."

"We played fifteen minutes of some zoo game. I seriously set an alarm. When the alarm went off, the game was done."

Barrie sighs and nods. "I figured it was something like that."

"Is there something specific Will wants me to do with the kids?"

"He just likes them to be outside."

"Barrie, it rained last Wednesday. We went outside when the rain quit, but you came to get them about ten minutes later."

"I know. I know." Barrie nods and grabs at my hand. "I'm sorry."

"We'll go outside," I promise my sister. "Go enjoy your night."

We do have fun. In fact, Avery and I have so much fun in the kitchen that Bryson eventually abandons his book and joins us. I'm not a teacher, and I hate math skills, but I step back and let the kids do most of the work. Recipes involve fractions, so they're practicing math skills. And they're working together, which is impressive. Avery asks Bryson to measure the shredded cheese for her, and Bryson has Avery use my manual can opener on the cream of chicken soup.

They get along most of the time, though kids will be kids. Sometimes Avery takes the opportunity to drop talk about something cool she gets to do that Bryson doesn't—

like the school skating party. And there are times when Bryson gets angry and pinches her or tries to get physical with her. Probably the same sorts of things Barrie and I did when we were kids living under the same roof.

The TV's off while we eat. I don't know if that's a rule in their house, but I'm not a big TV watcher. The kids seem to think it's my rule, so I let them. When we're finished, Bryson clears the table, Avery washes the dishes, and I put everything away. Before Bryson can get to the living room to turn the TV on and play the latest video game, I clear my throat and make noises like I'm drumming.

"Could I make a suggestion?"

"What's a sub-jegshun?" Bryson turns to look at me where I'm standing in the doorway.

"What, Aunt Mabry?" Avery ignores Bryson and watches me like I should, too.

"Let's go for a walk."

Both kids go for the idea, so within five minutes we're outside walking south on the sidewalk in front of my house.

"What can we do next?" Bryson tugs on my hand.

"What do you want to do next?"

I expect him to mention the video game.

"Go-karts."

"What?" Avery, walking on my other side, leans around me to look at him.

"You wanna drive go-karts?" I ask him.

"Can we?" His grin melts my heart. If he grinned at me like that and asked if he could have a puppy, I'd probably buy him two before Barrie came back.

"Where?" Avery sounds interested.

"By the skate place." From the tone of Bryson's voice, you would think he said duuuhhh.

Avery looks up at me quickly. He's right; I saw the go-kart track at Wolverine Park the day Barrie and I took him and Joel to skate.

"Can we?" Avery's eyes light up at the thought.

Funny. My belly flip flops at the thought. Sure, I like driving go-karts, but what I really like is the possibility of seeing the handy man there. *Twain.* It's been over a week since I made a fool of myself and fell in his parking lot and then freaked about the snake.

Okay, I would freak out about the snake all over again.

"Um. Yeah, but..."

I'm wondering if Will would be angry if I took the kids to drive go-karts. I never realized Will has issues with what I do with his kids. Then again, as I explained to Barrie, I usually do fun things with them that either involve some kind of exercise or some kind of education. Not on purpose. I'm not kissing up as a good babysitter. And I'm not over-the-top on either thing as what should be done. It's because it's fun to play games with the kids.

"Have you ever done it before?" I ask Avery.

She nods. "Last summer. Bryson rides with Mom."

That makes me feel a bit better about the idea.

"Let me text your mom."

I hate to bother her if she's all stretched out on a yoga mat, feeling Zen, sweating out her stress. And yet, I would hate to take the kids somewhere without her or Will's permission and have one of them end up injured.

"Text her!" Bryson jumps up and down. He's walking backwards now, oblivious to the spot where the sidewalk is buckled. I reach out calmly and steer him over the concrete ripple so he doesn't trip. Once we're all safely past the rough spot, I pull my phone from my pocket and text my sister.

CHAPTER SEVEN

Twain

Hattie and Craig race to the go-karts. Ethan tugs at my hand, anxious to be out there with the big kids. I can hear the other two bickering, but Harper pretends not to.

"No fair, Hattie!" Ethan yells. He drags me to the gate and grunts with anger at his sister. "I want that one!"

The go-kart he wants is red. But so are five others—identical to the one Hattie claims.

"Ethan." Harper reaches around me and drops her hand on Ethan's shoulder. "If you're going to be like this, we'll go home."

Ethan sighs, but he wisely decides to keep his mouth shut.

"You wanna drive?" I ask Harper.

"Of course," she answers, "but I'm going solo."

I laugh as she slips by me and Ethan and joins her older two at the karts.

"Guess it's you and me, kid." I look down at Ethan, not surprised to see he's champing at the bit to get out there.

The track isn't busy, and it's a nice evening with the setting sun at our backs and the sounds of cicadas surrounding us. Keith is out of town with Truman—some big hotel deal going down in Miami. More power to them. I'm happy to be here with the kids. Truman's ex-girlfriend is meeting us here to drop their son Ryle off, so we'll ride for a while and then maybe find something to eat.

"Aunt Mabry! I wanna yellow kart."

I spin around when I overhear the kid's voice behind me. There's only one Mabry I've ever met, and I hold my breath now, hoping...There she is. Same lithe, athletic body and same ponytail. She's wearing shorts tonight—modest denim shorts with a David Bowie t-shirt. She looks casual and beautiful all wrapped together.

"Hey." She smiles when she looks my way, and our eyes meet.

"Mabry." I nod, hoping my smile isn't that horrible, goofy grin I had when I was in high school. My mom once caught me trying to color over my senior picture with a black Magic Marker. There might have been alcohol and sibling bickering to blame.

"Twain." She grabs the kid's hand and rests her free hand on a young girl's shoulder. "Fancy seeing you here."

"You guys riding?" I nod toward the karts at the start line.

"Yeah."

"Go on." I nod again. Mabry frowns and looks around for a clerk to take her money. "It's cool."

The girl with her looks at her silently, but when Mabry nods, she hurries to claim a red kart. I hear another sigh from Ethan.

"We're riding together," Mabry says to me as she nods toward the little guy with her. "That okay?"

"You bet."

Ethan and I follow Mabry and her nephew to the karts. They grab a yellow one, as Ethan races to the red one behind Hattie. We buckle up, and then Steve—the guy who runs the karts—lets us loose. It's fun; the kids are laughing and having a good time. Harper and I are having fun, racing each other. She's yelling something at me about being careful with her baby, but I wave as Ethan and I fly by her on the first lap.

I can't watch them all the time, but Mabry and her nephew appear to be having fun when Ethan and I pass them. Her nephew is hollering at the girl with them, trash talking her. Sounds like my niece and nephews. When the five-minute ride is over, Ethan and I climb out, but he wants to ride again.

Normally, I would be all for it, but I feel a pull toward Mabry. I would love to talk to her, and barring that, I'd love to just watch her. Try explaining that to a five-year-old kid.

"C'mon, Ethan," Harper calls to her son. "Ride with me."

Ethan studies her for a moment and apparently decides it's more important to ride again than to have a red kart. He joins Harper, and I leave the track as Truman's ex approaches with Ryle.

"Jules." I give Truman's ex-girlfriend a stoic nod. I like her, always have. She's a nice girl, and she made Truman happy. They were together in college; Jules was pregnant when they broke up. Not sure if anyone else knows what happened between them, but I don't. Truman's never volunteered any information, never asked for advice, so I keep my questions and thoughts to myself.

"You sure you don't mind keeping Ryle tonight?" she asks quietly. Ryle is the spitting image of my brother, except for Julie's big green eyes. He's watching her now with those big eyes. Ryle doesn't say much; he's the quietest six-year-old I know.

"You kidding?" I wink at my nephew. "I'm puttin' this kid to work tomorrow."

At this, Ryle grins, but he ducks behind Jules. She tousles his hair and nods at me.

"Call me." She shrugs. "If…he needs anything."

"We'll be fine," I promise her. Jules thanks me, kisses the top of Ryle's head, and slowly walks away. I nod at the go-kart track, knowing he doesn't want to ride. He's timid—he'll only ride with me when the track is closed and just the two of us are out there. "You wanna ride?"

Ryle shakes his head. He presses close to the fence and wraps his fingers around the metal, content to stand with me and watch his cousins while I watch a pretty girl named Mabry.

She drives like she skated the first time I saw her here. Confident and smooth, fast enough that her ponytail swings behind her in the wind. She's smiling and talking, and her nephew seems to be chattering at her. I like that she doesn't seem to mind. She must like kids.

Becca liked the idea of kids, but she wasn't crazy about the real thing. Her older brother has a son that Becca only saw on holidays and birthdays. It baffled her that my family is always together. I should have known we weren't right for each other. We met at an auction at the country club. I was there just for kicks. Truman and I went because Mom and Dad were busy with another community function. Maybe I drank more than I thought that night since I asked for her number and then dated her for two years.

This time, Mabry rounds her nephew and the girl—I assume she's her niece—up when the race is over.

"Aunt Mabry, could we get ice cream before we go home?"

Mabry looks at me, deadpan, and then drops her gaze to the boy.

"Dude. Last week, you told your dad all we did was play video games. And now you talked me into go-karts, and you want ice cream. Your dad's never gonna let you hang out with me anymore."

The little boy just grins at her, and I see the moment she melts and gives in. Her shoulders sag, and she drops her head back with a groan of frustration.

"You can get ice cream on the Porch," I tell her as they near me. "Just sayin'."

"The Porch?"

"Back of the Cabin over there. Little ice cream and cookie shop."

"Got any margarita-flavored ice cream?" she asks hopefully. I recognize the look on her face as one Harper wears often. A little bit exhausted and amused. It's a beautiful look on a woman—that mix of love and wisdom.

"No, but I could buy you a drink."

She arches her eyebrows but shakes her head. "I can't with the kids."

I figured she would say that, so I only nod in response.

"Show me the Porch?"

"You bet."

CHAPTER EIGHT

MABRY

Avery and Bryson walk ahead of us, but I keep an eye on them. A dark-haired boy who looks to be around Bryson's age walks close to Twain. I notice Twain tousle the boy's hair, but neither of them speak. We're only about four steps away from the go-kart track when a little voice yells, "Uncle Twain!"

Twain pivots and walks backwards. He doesn't say anything, but he tips his head and waits. I look over my shoulder as the little guy who was riding with him hurries toward us.

"Can I have some ice cream?"

"Sure." Twain nods and reaches out to the kid. He looks at me when the kid zips right by him and runs to catch up with Bryson. "Snubbed."

"Your nephew?"

"Ethan." He nods. "That one's five. I have about seventeen more."

"You do not."

"This is Ryle." He touches the boy's shoulder. "My brother's son. He's six."

The boy looks up at Twain. I watch with awe as they have a full conversation with a shared look. When Twain nods, the boy takes off running to follow Ethan.

He grins and tucks his hands in his pockets. Unlike the first time I saw him, he's wearing khaki shorts. He's tan already, his legs just the right amount of beefy, well-carved muscle. The plain red t-shirt he wears is stretched tight over his shoulders, his brown hair a little unruly and curly and carefree.

Dreamy.

"'Kay. Not seventeen. But a few."

"You're probably a popular uncle. Working out here."

He purses his lips thoughtfully and ends up grinning and shrugging.

"Maybe."

The kids beat us to the Cabin, and then Ethan takes point and leads us around what looks like a wrap-around porch. Sure enough, there's a bustling ice cream shoppe there that I would never have seen if Twain hadn't mentioned it.

"What's your favorite?" he asks me.

"Rocky Road."

"You got it," he says with a grin. He disappears inside with the kids. I follow, but when he sees me pulling my cash from my pocket, he shakes his head. "My treat."

"You don't have to do that."

"I want to," he answers simply. Our eyes hold for a moment. The kids are chattering—even Avery is talking with the boys. I want to argue with him since he picked up the go-kart rides. But there's something about the way he's looking at me that makes me hold back. In my experience, guys who *look* like Twain don't *act* like him. I nod and break the eye contact, wondering if he's married. I glance at his left hand, relieved to not see a wedding band. But then again, I know that doesn't necessarily mean anything.

"I'll be outside," I tell him. He nods, smiles at me as I walk backwards to the door, and then turns to round up the kids as I go out.

I grab an open picnic table to wait. It's getting late; not much left of the sun but a strip of hot pink around the horizon. Barrie might even be home now. Just in case, I pull my phone from my pocket to call her. When she doesn't answer, I leave her a message. The kids race out to another table—all with ice cream bars—and Twain joins me as I put my phone down.

"Boyfriend?" He hands me a waffle cone filled with two giant scoops of Rocky Road ice cream and sits down on the table by me.

"Nope."

"Have one?"

"Nope."

"Want one?"

"Are you applying?"

"Maybe, Mabry."

I snort and roll my eyes. "Seriously?"

"Right." He nods. "I have no room to talk. My parents like literature."

"So, you're named after Mark Twain?"

"Yep." He leans forward and rests his elbows on his knees. "My sister's named after Harper Lee. And my brother after Truman Capote."

I like it. It makes me want to meet his parents, his family.

"And have you read Mark Twain?"

"Of course."

"Favorite?"

"Huck Finn, of course."

"Where did you go to college?"

When I glance at him, he's taking a bite of his ice cream bar—looks like vanilla ice cream, coated in chocolate and nuts. Good choice. I shiver when his lips close over the treat. Can't help but wonder what his lips would feel like on mine right now. Cool. Velvety, maybe? He catches me watching him, and I feel my cheeks flame with embarrassment.

"That your way of asking me if I went to college? And why if I did, I'm working here as a groundskeeper?"

Stunned by his direct question, I stare at him for a moment, unable to form a word to answer him.

"Sorry." He shakes his head and looks away. "Sore spot."

"Well, my next question was going to be what you majored in." I clear my throat and study my cone. The ice cream is already starting to melt. He watches me lick the top of it. "Since your parents are literature buffs."

"Business management," he answers. "But I like to read. I went to Illinois."

"Illini?"

"Yep."

"Nice."

He's got to be smart if he went to U of I. As curious as I am about him holding a business management degree and working out here as a groundskeeper, I decide not to ask. Little too early to talk about touchy subjects.

"You?"

"I'm a speech-language therapist," I tell him. "Went to school in Indiana."

That grin creeps over his face before he can hide it.

"What?" I straighten my shoulders and eye him suspiciously.

"Nothin'." He shakes his head, but he's chuckling. "It's just cute that you're a speech therapist. And your name is Mabry."

When he looks at me, I draw back and study him with a frown. "It's my mom's maiden name."

"You—" He nods at the cone in my hand. I feel it before I see it, the cold, sticky melted ice cream on my fingers.

Good grief. Could I do anything else to look stupid in front of this guy?

He reaches for me, and for a second, I think he's going to lick the ice cream off my fingers. Or maybe I just want him to. Instead, he hands me a napkin. I switch the cone to my right hand and ball the napkin in my sticky hand. When our eyes meet, I shrug and laugh at myself.

"So." He huffs a deep breath and looks at the kids gathered around the table in front of us. "Can I have your number?"

"Maybe."

He flicks his eyes at me and gives me that charming grin when he sees that I'm teasing him.

"For the record?" he says.

"Mm-hmm." I arch my eyebrows and wait for him to continue.

"I think it's pretty."

"You think what's pretty?" I can barely say the words over the swarm of butterflies in my belly and fluttering in my throat.

"Well, you, for sure," he says with a nonchalant shrug. "Your name."

"I like yours, too," I tell him with a nod. "And you are kind of cute."

"So, is that a yes, Mabry?"

"What's there to do on a date around here?" I ask as I lick my cone again.

"Not much." He plays along. "Good bowling alley across town."

"Surprised there isn't one here."

"Lots not big enough," he answers immediately. "Can't do that or a golf course."

CHAPTER NINE

Twain

"Aren't you going to write it down?" she asks me after she rattles off her number.

"I'll remember it."

"Will you?" She tips her head at me in disbelief.

I have a head for numbers, and I do plan to call her. I want to see her again, so I'm not going to leave it to chance. I'll remember her number. Eyes locked with hers, I simply nod.

Mabry breaks the eye contact and looks around. The kids are giggling at the table in front of us; even Ryle is grinning. Hattie has told me he does talk when there aren't adults around, but it's still good to see him looking the way a kid is supposed to look.

"Where's Jaws?"

"What?" I jerk my attention from the kids and back to her.

"I assume he's, like, the guard dog for the whole...park." She nods her head to the side to indicate the grounds.

I snort. "Hardly."

"Hardly a guard dog? Or hardly around here?"

"Oh, he's around all the time," I say with a nod. "But he's not mean."

"Except to birds."

"Occasionally, yes."

She smiles as she continues to work on her ice cream. I've polished mine off by now.

"You're close to your nephews, aren't you?"

"Yeah. And there's more." I watch her study the steaks of melted ice cream that have coated her cone again. "You need to lick faster."

She flicks her eyes my way and laughs softly.

"I feel like a little kid." She crunches a bit of her cone and meets my eyes for a second. "My niece is having a birthday party here next week."

"Good."

Always good to know there's more business, but now, business is the last thing on my mind.

"Are you around on Saturday afternoons?"

I'm always around, but I don't share that with her.

"I'll make it a point to be."

"Yeah? Do you skate?"

"Yep."

"Backwards?"

"I do. I can even do figure eights."

"So, if there were moonlight skates—are they called moonlight skates?—you could skate backwards and hold my hands?"

"Yep. And we call them couple skates. There usually aren't many at a kids' birthday party in the middle of the afternoon."

"Too bad I don't know anyone to bribe so I could change that."

She's flirting openly now. I haven't done this for a long time. I forgot how fun it is to flirt with a pretty woman. When Becca left, the idea of women exhausted me.

"I might know a guy," I tell her.

"Good."

"What about you? Did you decide to have your party here?"

"I think I'm a little too old for a birthday party."

"You're never too old for fun."

"True." She nods. "Maybe I will. Maybe Barrie and I can do a girls' night out. I haven't seen a lot of my old friends since I moved back. I'm not sure too many of them live around here anymore."

"So, you're originally from Basset?"

"Yeah. I lived here as a kid. My parents moved us to Springfield when I was a sophomore. Barrie moved back to be with her husband. I went away to school. Just now coming back."

I'm about to ask her why she came back, but her phone buzzes on the table. She grabs it quickly and swipes the screen.

"Hey."

I climb off the table and head over to join the kids to give her some space and see what's got all the kids giggling.

"Uncle Twain." Ethan slides closer to me on the bench seat.

"Careful, dude." I pat his leg. "You don't want a splinter."

"Bryson burped the alphabet."

Just the recap stirs the giggles up again. Mabry's niece rolls her eyes, but there's a small smile on her face.

"Nice."

"Can we go skating?" Ethan asks me.

"Not tonight."

"Please?"

"Hey." Mabry appears at the table. "I just talked to your mom, guys. She's home."

I wonder if Mabry is babysitting, or if, like me, she just enjoys spending time with the kids. I wonder where her sister was. Where does Mabry live? So many things I want to ask her, but it's not the right time.

"Do we have to go?" Her niece asks.

"Yep." Mabry nods.

"Can we come back again?"

"Sure."

The girl climbs to her feet, and Bryson—apparently, he and Ethan have already become friends—follows suit, though grudgingly. I know how he feels. I stand up, wishing I could walk her to her car. Without an audience. Kiss her goodbye, although even without an audience, it's probably too soon.

"So, you're gonna call me."

"I am."

"What's my number?"

I'm not sure she's impressed when I say it back to her, but she is surprised.

"Goodnight, Twain," she says with a cute smirk.

"Goodnight, Mabry."

I watch them walk back up past the Porch and around to the front of the building. Mabry has a hand on each of the kids' shoulders. Looks like Bryson is talking her ear off.

"Are you gonna marry her?" Ethan tugs at my hand.

"What?"

"Can I be the ring bear?"

If Hattie had asked something like this at Ethan's age, I wouldn't have blinked. She was all girl with her ballet slippers and fingernail polish. Ethan doesn't usually pay attention to details outside of himself, so his question catches me off guard.

"Bearer," I correct him.

"Yeah." He nods. "Can I?"

"I'm not gonna marry her," I tell him.

"You should."

Shocked, I turn to look at Ryle. He's looking up at me with his heart in his big eyes. Chocolate ice cream outlines his lips.

"I should?"

He narrows his eyes at me for a second, like he's really thinking about it, and then he nods.

"What do you guys know about getting married?" I plop back down on the bench between them.

"She makes you coffee in the morning," Ethan announces.

"Oh. Okay. That would be nice."

"I drink coffee with my mom." Ryle's frown is pensive. It kind of hurts that he can't tell me what he knows about marriage. "You have to tell her she's pretty."

"Yeah?" I lean back on the table and fold my arms over my chest. "How do you know that, Ryle?"

Does Jules have a boyfriend? Does Truman know?

"Grampa tells Gramma she's pretty," he answers with a shrug.

He's right. My parents are still in love after thirty-eight years of marriage. I suppose Ryle could do worse than watching my dad as a family man.

CHAPTER TEN

MABRY

"Ryle thinks I should marry you."

I flick my gaze at my phone and then look back at the road. Slowing to a stop behind a pickup truck at a red light, I look at my phone again. The number isn't familiar to me, but I know who it is. I know his voice already, and both that knowledge and his voice chase warm tingles just under my skin.

"Who is this?"

"Twain."

While I want to tease him, pretend he's got the wrong number, I can't help the snort of laughter.

"You're playing me."

"What if you had the wrong number? You can't propose

over the phone to someone the first time you call. You might have dialed a crazy old cat lady."

"Are you a cat lady?"

"No. But that's beside the point."

"It's not a proposal. It was an observation made by a very, very quiet six-year-old boy."

"Hmm."

"It sparked a good discussion."

"You didn't." I ease my foot off the brake as the light turns green. It's been a long day. When I left the hospital minutes ago, I was tired. Now I'm feeling revived.

"What?"

"You did not talk to your nephews about the birds and the bees."

"No." He sounds like he thinks I'm crazy, even if I'm not a cat lady. "I asked them what they know about marriage."

"And?"

"Well, Ethan says, if we were married, you would have to make me coffee in the mornings."

"That's pretty sexist," I say, but I'm smiling. We haven't even been on a date, and I'm driving home from work, talking to this guy about marriage.

"Yeah, well, his brother thought I had a girlfriend just to clean my house, but that's a whole other story."

Maybe, but now the story I want to hear is about the girlfriend.

"Okay." I push that question to the back of my mind as I navigate the streets to get home. "So, what did Ryle say about marriage?"

"That every day I have to tell you that you're pretty."

"Hmm." I nod. "Smart kid."

"Yeah. He said Grampa tells Grama that every day."

"Secret to a long life together," I agree.

"So what do you say?"

"I think it's a bit soon to get married," I answer. "I mean, you haven't even bought me dinner. No goodnight kiss. I'm not making coffee for a guy who doesn't kiss me goodbye."

His laughter rumbles through the phone, and I'm grinning like an idiot as I drive. I don't even care that the woman next to me when I stop at the next intersection is looking at me.

"I know a fun place for dinner."

"Are you asking me out?"

"I am."

"Okay."

"Ever been to Harvey's?"

"No. But my sister and her husband go there."

Barrie loves the place. From all accounts, it's a funky burger bar with crazy colorful decor, delicious burgers, and milkshakes. And, of course, a full bar.

"Can I pick you up?"

I give him my address, wondering if he's writing it down. Probably not. This guy is like a wolf in sheep's clothing. He seems so laid back, you'd think he wouldn't pay any attention to detail. But apparently, he does.

"Six o'clock?" he asks me. I glance at the clock on my dashboard. That gives me about an hour to get ready for the first date I've been on in the better part of a year. Normally, that would make me balk, demand more time. Tonight, I barely catch myself before asking what's going to take him so long.

"Perfect," I tell him.

"Not gonna tell Ryle we're going out," he says. "You know, in case he tells my family we're getting married. They'll think we eloped."

"Goodbye, Twain."

I DON'T KNOCK MYSELF OUT OVER WHAT TO WEAR after my quick shower. It's not that I don't want to impress Twain. It's more that he seems a little deeper than skinny jeans and heavy eyeliner. I do grab a pair of jeans, though they're boyfriend cut, and they sit loose on my hips. The cuffs are rolled; I slip my bare feet into a pair of red loafer sneakers. And pull on a white knit top. It's simple, and while it's comfortable for me, it feels like the sort of outfit Twain would appreciate.

I swipe on a few strokes of mascara, blow my hair just a little dry, and then pull it back in a loose twist. There's a knock at my door as I flip the bathroom light off. A glance at my phone tells me it's six on the dot.

"Hey." I pull the door open, relieved to see he's dressed casual in faded denim that looks soft over his thighs and a light blue knit shirt.

"Hi." His voice is deep and smooth, and his grin inviting and warm. How is he single? And how did I get lucky enough to fall on my butt in front of him just a week ago? "Ready?"

"Yeah. Let me just..." I twist around to grab my wristlet purse and keys from the end table by the sofa and then step outside with him.

"So." He follows me to the passenger side of his truck and reaches for the door handle. "For the record? I do think you're pretty."

Unable to hold back the grin, I bite my lip and duck my head.

"Still not ready to make you coffee every morning."

He laughs, and when I look up at him, he leans in and kisses my cheek.

"'kay, I might *bring* you coffee," I tell him as he pulls my door open for me. We're teasing, but teasing about what marriage is with him feels different from other dates. Even if these are his nephews' ideas about marriage.

Once I'm in the truck, Twain closes the door and comes around to his side to get in. He starts the truck and pulls away from the curb, Tim McGraw serenading us as he drives.

"So, do you babysit your niece and nephew a lot?"

I'm about to ask him about his family—if he's close to his siblings—when he hits me with the question.

"Mmm." I nod my head back and forth. "I guess. But I don't feel like it's babysitting. It's more that I love getting to hang out with them."

From the corner of my eye, I see him nod.

"Barrie has an evening yoga class," I explain. "So, it's time for her. Will's a great dad, but I've been trying to use that night as a chance to hang with them."

"But you can't play video games?"

I laugh softly. "They limit the kids' time on gaming. Last week when I watched them, it rained. So, we played our allotted time of video games and then I broke out the good, old board games."

"Favorite?"

"Monopoly."

"Eh." He looks at me and rolls his eyes. "That was always Harper's favorite, too. Just because she always cheated, so she always won."

"Define cheating." I turn sideways so I can see him better.

"She said since she was the oldest, she should be the banker. She stole money all the time."

"What piece were you?"

"The car," he says like I should know without asking. "You?"

"The dog."

"But you're scared of Jaws?"

"I'm not scared of Jaws."

"Right."

"Okay, so I had just fallen on my butt and put on a show for you. Bryson was talking about lizards. And you were just...."

"What?" When he looks at me, the corners of his mouth are tipped up in a small grin. "I was what?"

"Well, just there. Oozing cute and charm. And then Joel finds a snake—"

"Wait." He lifts his right hand from the steering wheel and holds it up to stop me. "Let's revisit that."

"What? The snake? Do you like snakes?"

"I have nothing against them," he shrugs, "but no. Let's revisit me oozing cute and charm."

"Well." I shrug. "You were. I looked like a klutz."

"I'm just unaware that I ooze anything, really, let alone cute and charm. I wanna know how I do it. You know, in case this marriage doesn't work out. Might need it next time."

It's effortless—the way he makes me feel. Happy. Safe. Comfortable like I've known him forever. Intrigued, because I haven't, and I want to know more. I want to know everything.

"What's your favorite?"

"Board game?" He sighs and drums his fingers on the steering wheel. He drops his right hand to rest on his leg. "Probably Sorry."

"Something tells me Harper didn't like that one."

"No, she didn't. Truman and I were a pain."

"Oh, I bet you were."

"You just said I'm charming."

"Not to a sister, I bet."

"You get along with your sister?"

"Now," I answer with a laugh. "Usually. We had our fair share of fights when we were kids."

I look out the windshield when he flips his turn signal on and pulls into the parking lot by Harvey's. The lot is packed. The patio looks like there might be five people to each car.

"Hungry?" He pops his seatbelt and opens his door.

Our eyes meet. I am. I had a chicken salad sandwich for lunch, and that was at eleven. But right now, with our eyes locked, I'm thinking about the brush of his lips over my cheek earlier.

"Yes."

"Let's go."

CHAPTER ELEVEN

TWAIN

The wait for a table is thirty minutes. Everybody in Harvey's knows me, but it's not like in the movies, where I can go in and flash a folded bill at a maître de and get a table just like that. Little bit more like we walk in and decide to go to the bar for a drink while we wait, and every person there hollers at me to say hi.

Mabry doesn't seem intimidated. When Hap Wiley asks what she wants to drink, she orders a draft beer and sits on a stool, familiar with the whole scene. Hap draws her beer and then gets mine without asking. He slides both glasses over the bar to us, nods at me, and moves on to his next customer.

"Seems like you're pretty well known here," she says as she picks up her glass.

I nod and shrug. Most people in Basset do know me. Some because they voted against me expanding the park, and some because they're regulars at one attraction or another there. Mabry is sizing me up over her glass. I'm not ready to tell her I own the grounds, the attractions. The whole complex. When I told Becca, she blinked, and dollar signs rolled up in her eyes like lucky sevens on a slot machine.

Mabry isn't a thing like Becca, but I'm still me, and I decided after processing Becca's greed and conditional love, I need to be a bit more discerning with women I date. I'm done with the partying college days. Done with the casual hookups—not that there were ever many. I'm ready to settle down. And of all the women I've bumped into since Becca left, Mabry's the only one to get my attention.

I watch her sip her beer and then rub her lips together. I brought Becca here once. She ordered a glass of wine and drank it all and then told her best friend later—where I was sure to overhear—that it was cheap wine, and the place was too casual for her.

"So." Mabry clears her throat. Someone pushes up beside her on her right to order, but she doesn't flinch. Doesn't look away from me. There are eight big screen TVs strategically placed around the bar, though music pumps around the room. The song right now is familiar to me, because I hear it here, but it's not country, so I don't know it. Still, it's good background music for a first date. It's an easy, soft beat. Mabry's moving to the music so smoothly, I'm guessing she doesn't realize she's doing it.

I brace myself for her question. *Why does everyone know you?* Why would everyone know the groundskeeper or janitor—or whatever she thinks I am—at Wolverine Park?

"You said your nephew thought your girlfriend was around to clean your house."

I swallow a mouthful of beer and laugh as I put my glass down. Mabry arches an eyebrow at me.

"He did say that. Ex-girlfriend."

"Is that why she's an ex? Because of what he said?"

"No." I shake my head. "We just wanted different things out of life."

"Like what?"

"Well, for starters, she wasn't crazy about the idea of having kids."

"Mmm." She flinches and looks away. "Gotcha."

"She has a brother and nephew, but she's not close to them. I think that made it hard for her to get that I'm close to my family."

"How long did you date?"

"Two years."

"Long time to date when you want different things out of life." She meets my eyes as she sips again from her glass.

"I know. You get complacent. Make excuses about the

things that you know aren't right. Because sometimes it's easier than change."

"Very true."

We sit in companionable silence for a while, drinking our beers. Mabry's a people watcher. I love that about her. She watches people with interest, and she smiles a lot, like she's genuinely happy and easily moved by other people's happiness.

When our table is ready, I follow her to the patio. It's a bit quieter outside, though we can still hear the music. I wonder if she likes to dance. After watching her skate that first day, I bet she does.

"What about you?" I ask her.

She's looking at her menu when she answers me. "Eww. The Harvey burger."

"Don't do it, unless you have a stomach of steel."

She flicks her gaze up to mine and frowns. "You've tried it?"

I nod. "On a dare."

"Really?" She grins at me. "I'm not sure I would've taken you for one to do a dare."

"Truman." I shrug. "I'm not, really. But Truman."

"What does that mean?"

"He's my kid brother," I answer simply. "If he dares me to do something, better believe I'm gonna do it."

"But peanut butter and jelly on a burger?"

"What do you like on yours?"

"Pickles. Tomatoes and mustard."

"But not ketchup?"

"No."

"Weird." I roll my eyes. "So, you don't have a boyfriend now—"

"Mmm." She bites her lip. "Kind of seeing someone now."

"Yeah?"

"He's kinda cute. Likes Huck Finn."

"Any exes your new guy should worry about?"

"Exes," she shrugs, "but none to worry about." Before she can say more, our waiter—yep, I know him, too—shows up for our order. Mabry asks for a classic cheeseburger with pickle and tomato on the side. I order my usual bacon cheeseburger and fries.

"Ever been in love?"

"Did your nephews tell you to ask me that?"

"What do they know about love?"

"Sounds like plenty," she says with a smile. "Yeah. I guess so."

"What happened?"

"I don't know. First time I was seventeen. We went to different colleges. That was that. Dated in college. Lived with someone for seven months. Found out we just weren't compatible. He got lazy. Didn't want to do much outside of TV. I like to be on the go."

I nod, because I've only known her a week, and I see that already.

"Ever talk to him?"

"No. We parted as friends, but I haven't talked to him in years."

I finish my beer as she picks hers up. She's got a swallow left.

"Should've ordered another."

"He'll bring another round."

She narrows her eyes at me. "How do you know that?"

"I know him," I hedge. It feels dishonest not to tell her I own the biggest attraction in town, but I'm not sure I'm *ready* to tell her. Still, I don't know how to change the subject without being rude.

"You know everyone."

"Small town."

"Not that small," she argues. "But I guess you probably see a lot of people when you're working, don't you? That place is a goldmine. The parking lots look like new car lots sometimes."

Her words are like a quick slip of a knife. In and out of my gut before I can register what happened. I don't think she meant it in a greedy way; after all, it's just a saying —*something is a goldmine.*

But after Becca tried to remake me into someone she felt comfortable being seen with, it's hard to shrug off Mabry's comment.

CHAPTER TWELVE

Mabry

"Never?" I ask him.

The burger was delicious, and the milkshakes look tasty. But I didn't want to mix one with the beer I started with. Maybe next time. I think there'll be a next time. I like him. He's not just easy on the eyes. He's easy. Comfortable. Like, comfortable in his skin which makes it easy to be myself around him.

The crowd has cleared out a little. Lots of people have waved at him and said something. It's like I'm with a local celebrity. But then again, he's friendly and easy to talk to. I'm sure he does see a lot of people at the park, and it makes sense that he talks to all of them.

The music tonight has been a great mix of indie, alternative, and even some blues. Our conversation has bounced all over from family to dating to the value of a dollar and back to family. Twain finds it funny that

Barrie used to call me Maybe Baby. I assure him it's not because I'm indecisive. But because Barrie was a pain in my butt back in the days when we were in grade school and living under the same roof. He's asked why I'm named with my mom's maiden name, since Barrie's the older daughter. And he only nodded and smiled when I told him Barrie is named after our dad's dad—Barry.

"Well." He purses his lips and rubs his chin. We've finished our beers, but neither of us has made a move to leave. I'm in no hurry to end the date, but I have to admit I'm already thinking about our goodbye. And hoping for a kiss. "Maybe once."

"Once." I shake my head. "Barrie used to dare me to do all kinds of things just to get me in trouble."

"Harper did that," he says with a nod. "With me *and* Truman."

"But you only dared Truman to do something once?"

"Well, I mean, it was a doozy."

"What was it?"

Twain sighs and sits back. "I dared him to kidnap the high school principal's dog. And demand a ransom."

Stunned, I can only stare at him. I fumble for my half full glass of water and take a sip. "For what reason?"

"Well, the whole student body was in trouble for bad sportsmanship. There was a group at a football game that was doing this mean cheer. So, we all got in trouble the following Monday. Mr. Petty was going to cancel a big school dance."

"And why did that matter to you?"

"Because Alicia Gephardt was going with me to the dance."

Interesting. The funny thing is, Twain is still smiling, and that smile is still oozing charm. And I still like it. Him. Even more than before this date started.

"Why was that so important to you?"

"Because she was the hottest girl in the class."

It doesn't seem like his style, but then I'll give him the benefit of the doubt. Most of us change a lot between our senior years of high school and our thirties.

"Wow." I laugh and roll my eyes. "So, did Truman do it? Kidnap the dog?"

"Yep."

I wince, knowing Twain's going to tell me that Truman got caught.

"The ransom was reinstating the dance?" I ask.

He nods. "You ready to get outta here?"

We stand and exit the patio through the gate outside. As we walk to his truck, our fingers link, as if we've been doing this for years.

"How much trouble did he get into?"

"Well, he had a week of in-school suspension."

"That's it?"

"We took care of the dog," he says as if that explains everything. "Not like we water-boarded it."

We stop at the front of his truck.

"But, no, that wasn't it. My dad grounded Truman for three months."

"Ouch."

"And he grounded me for six months, because even though Truman didn't rat me out, Dad figured out I was responsible."

"Your senior year? You were grounded for six months?"

"No going out for a month. I could leave the house to work. And when I did get to finally go out, I didn't get my car keys back for a long time. Had to bum rides from everybody."

"How did he know you were involved?"

Twain shrugs and laughs, and his eyes twinkle. He looks like he's fifteen, just a carefree kid, loving life. I think about kissing him again, but I look away quickly, so he won't see it in my eyes.

"I guess you just looked guilty?" I ask. "Probably always full of mischief when you were a kid."

"I thought I was charming." He reaches for me and cups my chin. Turns my face back to look at him.

"Fine line sometimes."

Suddenly, we're standing close enough that I feel the heat from his body. I breathe in his cologne, something minty, a little sweet.

"You like bad boys?" He quirks an eyebrow at me.

"I like this one," I tell him. Before I can stop myself, my fingers are on his face. My finger brushing over the dimple on his chin. "I'm sorry, but this is adorable."

"Mabry," he says, his voice gruff, "most guys don't want to be adorable. But I can live with it if it's coming from you."

"Yeah?" I let my eyes roam over his face. His lips are parted, and I see the tiny chip in his front tooth—compliments of Harper when she was thirteen and he was ten, and they were playing pitch and catch. I almost feel like I know them just from the stories he's shared with me tonight.

When our eyes meet again, he leans in and brushes his soft, warm lips over mine. It's a whole lot like the kiss he put on my cheek earlier tonight. But it's a whole lot more than that, too. It's a summer afternoon, sitting on the side of the pool, legs in the cold water. It's a glass of fresh lemonade on a hot day. It's your favorite song on repeat with no one around to talk and make you miss it.

He's bought me dinner and kissed me goodnight. Hope he doesn't tell Ryle that, or we might have some sort of crazy arranged marriage in the works.

CHAPTER THIRTEEN

Twain

"What're you doing tomorrow?"

I look down from my spot on the ladder as my brother approaches the side of the skating rink. Cleaning out the gutters is not my favorite job, but it beats cleaning the bathrooms and I do that one, too, when needed.

"I dunno."

Truman frowns up at me and lifts his hand to shield his eyes from the sun.

"Why?" I ask as I look back up at the gutter.

"You cut that big tree down there, you wouldn't have so much to clean out of the gutters."

"I like the tree," I answer. Some days, time spent with my family is a repeat of every conversation we ever have.

Harper wants to find me a desk where I can put out a name plate and stare at a computer screen and wear suits. Truman wants me to cut this Maple tree down and pave the gravel lot at the rink. My parents want me to settle down and get married so I can start a family.

Mom claims she wants that for my happiness—as if I can't be happy out here with all of this on my own. I tease her that she just wants more grandchildren so she can stay busy with them and not deal with my dad.

Thinking about Mom and Dad and the whole when-are-you-going-to-settle-down question makes me think of Mabry. Hanging out with her at Harvey's the other night. The way her laughter made me happy. Swapping stories about our siblings and the trouble we got into when we were kids. Kissing her goodnight. There was the kiss as we left the restaurant. Soft and sweet. And I kissed her again when I took her home. Still sweet, but that one was a little bit more involved.

I flex my fingers now, remembering the feel of her hair in my hands. Her hands on my shoulders and her fingertips drawing a line under my chin, spreading over my neck.

"Dad and I are going golfing. Come with us."

Truman's bluntly delivered invitation snaps me out of those thoughts.

"What time?"

"Seven fifteen tee time."

Dad and Truman golf often. I go occasionally. While I enjoy it and can sometimes play well enough to not embarrass myself, I'm not always up for hours with my dad and brother. There are times they hash out business deals and ideas on the course, and I find myself considering bonking one or both of them on the head with my seven iron.

"Okay."

"You haven't gone with us in—" Truman stops talking and just stares at me. "What?"

"I said okay."

"Really? You're just gonna agree to go? No argument?"

"Just like that." I shrug and laugh at the disgruntled look on his face.

"Wow." He takes a deep breath and then his shoulders sag. "I came out here ready to argue with you."

"Mom send you?"

"No." From the corner of my eye, I see him shrug.

I sneak a peek at him as I climb down the ladder and scoot it a few feet to the right only to climb up and start again.

"You know you could hire this out?" He leans on the building.

"Yep."

"You could hire out just about everything you do here," he mutters.

"And then what would I do?"

"Dad and I are talking about building some storage units on that plot of land he bought out on East Maine."

"And?" I shrug. "What's that got to do with me?"

"Go in on it with us."

"And then what? Would I be building the actual storage units? Or manning a desk for people to come in and rent space?"

"You're a pain."

"I like being outside. Sue me."

"Ryle said you got him ice cream the other night."

I still my hands, both full of the helicopters from the Maple and turn my head to look at him.

"Is that a problem?"

"Nope." He gives me a dramatic shrug.

Our eyes hold for a few seconds, but when he doesn't say more, I turn my attention back to the gutter.

"Ryle says you have a girlfriend."

I bark out a laugh and back down the ladder again to study my brother's face.

"Is that what this is about?"

"You do." His grin brings to mind afternoon bike rides and homemade ramps and skinned knees. "Who is she?"

"She's none of your business," I answer.

"Seriously? You're gonna play that game?"

"It's new, Truman. I don't care to share anything about her yet."

He huffs out a sigh and rolls his eyes. "What's her name?"

"Asked and answered." I start back up the ladder. "You need something?"

"Ryle wants to go roller skating."

Well, that hits me like a shovel between the eyes. Ryle wants to skate? Sometimes the kid is afraid of his own shadow. He'll only do the go-karts when the place is closed, and we're the only ones here. And I've never been able to talk him into skating.

I'm excited that my nephew wants to try something new. But I can't help but wonder why today of all days—when Mabry is going to be here with her niece. Unless the boys talked about it and Ryle wants to skate today because Bryson will be here. As much as I'm not ready to share Mabry with anyone—not ready to share the idea of Mabry, even—I climb the ladder with a weight off my shoulders. Ryle's decision to try skating, his desire to hang out with friends, makes me feel good.

"So, where is he?" I twist around on the ladder and look around for my nephew.

"Jules is meeting me out here. He's gonna hang out with me today."

I snort. "You're skating?"

"Yep."

Like me, Truman and Harper grew up on skates. Truman's slick and smooth on skates, but he doesn't enjoy it. He'll hate wasting time on the rink this afternoon. I wish he would just relax and have fun; it would be good for Ryle.

"How's Jules?" I ask to distract myself. I might have opinions about Ryle and his needs, but I'm not a parent, so I don't lecture or even advise my brother about his son. When Truman doesn't answer immediately, I look down at him again. He glances at me and shrugs.

"I think she's seeing someone."

Our eyes meet for a second. He looks away before I can be sure, but he doesn't seem happy about it.

The sounds of cars from the lot draws my attention.

"What time is it?"

Truman shrugs. "Did she say anything to you when she dropped Ryle off the other night?"

"Jules?" I ask him. "No. Just told me to call if Ryle needed anything."

"Got another ladder? I'll help."

That's new. Truman's never offered to help with anything before.

"Nope. Go wait for Ryle."

"You really gonna golf with us tomorrow?"

"I really am," I tell him.

"What's her name?" he asks me again.

"Ask Ryle."

CHAPTER FOURTEEN

"Aunt Mabry, c'mon!"

Avery grabs my hand when the guy playing the music at her party announces it's time for the Hokey Pokey. It's not Cliffie today; I don't recognize this guy. I haven't seen Twain today either, although we've texted some. We've talked on the phone once since our date the other night, and we've texted often the past few days. We're at the fun, exciting stage of dating—we've been out once, and we both know we enjoyed the date and want to go out again.

I usually work with stroke or brain injury patients, as well as cancer patients who have swallowing difficulties due to radiation treatments. Seeing improvement with each of them is rewarding, but it's a heavy job, and sometimes it's heartbreaking.

The last few days at work, having Twain and the date and the kisses tucked away in a box in my head, has made me feel a little lighter. Finding texts on my phone or knowing we might talk on the phone when I get home makes me happy, even when I'm frustrated for my patients and even grieving with families who end up losing loved ones to those major health events.

We're about a half hour into Avery's party, and so far, I've stayed upright. Barrie and Will have managed to do so, though Will's had a few close calls and has careened into the rail once. I'm not sure about the Hokey Pokey, but my niece drags me out on the floor, so I go with it. Barrie laughs and waves at me from the railing where she stands with Bryson. She points at him and then at me, and I realize she's telling me Bryson wants to do the Hokey Pokey. Avery is surrounded by her friends, so I skate over to the rail to get Bryson.

"Can Ryle come out with us?" he asks when I reach for his hand.

"What?" I look to his right, surprised to find Twain's nephew standing a few feet away. When he sees me look at him, he flashes me a sloppy grin. With a laugh, I look around for Twain. I don't see him, but the guy with Ryle looks enough like Twain, that he has to be his brother. "Sure. Are you Truman?"

The guy—he's good-looking, too, but prettier and more polished than Twain—snaps his head around to look at me suspiciously.

"I am."

"Hey, I'm Mabry." I offer my hand, relieved when he takes it to shake, albeit reluctantly. "I'm a friend of Twain's."

Like I flipped a switch in his head, his eyes light up and he smiles. The skin around his eyes crinkles a bit, but not like Twain's, and his brown eyes are suddenly warm and inviting like his brother's.

"So, it's you," he says so softly, I almost don't hear him.

"Can I go with Bryson, Daddy?" Ryle tips his head back to look at Truman.

"He's been on skates once," Truman tells me. "Like. Now."

I laugh softly. After all, that's what started me on this new adventure—my nephew's introduction to roller skating.

"It's okay," I promise Truman. "Bryon's a rookie, too."

"You don't mind?" he asks me.

"Daddy, you, too." Ryle tucks his hand inside Truman's. I hold my breath, wondering what he'll do. Ryle still stares at him with those big, beautiful eyes. I would have buckled under that pressure instantly.

"You want me to Hokey Pokey?" Truman looks down at the kid. He laughs softly, but he nods. "Okay. Let's go."

The four of us skate back out to the black circle in the middle of the rink. Avery sees me with Bryson and flashes me a pretty smile, but she stays with her friends. We put our right foot and left foot and hands in and turns ourselves around. The boys struggle with every move and end up on the floor more often than standing on skates. But they're giggling. Ryle watches Truman closely, his eyes following his every move. His mouth frozen in a happy smile.

Truman handles himself well on skates, making me wonder about Twain. I know he's working today, but I had hoped I'd get to see him before the party's over. It won't be long before we go back to the party room to do Avery's cake and presents.

"That was great!" Barrie announces when we skate to the rail. Bryson and Ryle grab on and wrap their arms around the wood as if they'll drown if they let go. Truman does a smooth hockey stop, and the boys look at him in awe. "Way to shake it all about, Mabe."

"I haven't done that in at least twenty years," Truman says as he scrubs his hands over his head. He wears his dark hair shorter and neater than Twain's. I decide there's not enough there to tangle my fingers in for goodnight kisses. Not like Twain has.

"Me neither," I answer.

"You're a natural." Truman meets my eyes.

"She's a pro—"

"Stop it." I swing my hip sideways to bump my sister and shut her up.

"You look familiar." Barrie studies Truman's face with an embarrassing intensity. She's going to say something to make me look stupid. I just know it.

"Truman."

"You look like that guy—"

"Isn't it about time to do Avery's cake?" I interrupt her.

"Oh." She looks over her shoulder at the concession stand. "I think we have a few minutes, but I guess we should go check the room. Make sure I didn't forget anything."

"I'll be there in a minute."

Barrie grabs Will by the arm on her way to the concession stand, leaving me alone with Truman and the two little guys.

"You're seeing my brother, aren't you?" Truman asks with a totally simple normal smile. So, why does his question make me nervous? Like it's loaded with meaning I can't begin to discern. "Twain."

I'm not sure how to answer that. Yes, I want to say I'm *seeing* Twain. But maybe Twain isn't ready for that. One good date doesn't necessarily mean we're *seeing* each other. Is Truman planning to report back to Twain?

"We've gone out," I tell him, wondering if that's understating what we're doing. What if Truman tells

Twain I sound less than excited about our date? I'm smiling, but with Truman watching me so intently, I wonder if I'm selling it. Or if I look fake.

"What's your name?"

"Oh man." Twain's voice booms from behind us. I sag with relief. While I think Truman wouldn't mean any harm between us, I'm glad Twain's here just the same. "This is my worst nightmare."

Truman smirks at him over my shoulder.

"This guy bothering you?" Twain brushes his hand over my upper back and then slides it lower to my waist.

"Ryle and I just did the Hokey Pokey with her and Bryson."

Twain laughs and looks down at the boys. He puts his hands up for high fives and nods with enthusiasm when they boys oblige.

"Leave it to you to Hokey Pokey with her." Twain rolls his eyes. We adults laugh, but the boys are clueless.

"Truman, this is Mabry." Twain moves his hand from my waist. I miss the presence immediately, but I don't say anything. "Please behave yourself around her. Mabry, I see you've met Truman. My sympathy."

Truman winces and laughs. "I always behave myself," he says, but he looks at me when he says it.

"And pigs fly," Twain mumbles.

"Nuh-uh." Ryle's deep voice draws a hearty laugh from both brothers.

"It's nice to meet you, Mabry." Truman sounds sincere.

"Mabry!" Barrie's yell carries further and louder when the song stops and the DJ makes an announcement for Avery's party.

"I'll talk to you later," Twain says to me.

I look at him closely for the first time since he walked in. He's got jeans on, but he's wearing Vans. So he must be done working for the day. Did he pack a change of clothes so he could come in and find me here?

"What? No!" I shake my head. "We're doing the party. Can Ryle come with us?"

Truman looks at his son and back at me. Bryson and Ryle stand side to side, like Siamese twins.

"Ryle, buddy, you can see him later—"

"Seriously. Let him come with us. Bryson will love it."

"Are you sure?"

"Come with us." I reach for Bryson's hand, but I look back and forth between Twain and Truman. "Please."

This time when Truman looks at Ryle and the kid wags his eyebrows hopefully, Truman gives in. They fall in line behind me as I lead them through concessions to the party rooms. Bryson, hopped up on sugar and adrenaline, gets ahead of me just as a little girl with a cup of ice cream walks in front of him. The ice cream cup goes flying as Bryson and the girl crash to the floor. I'm moving too fast to stop, and I don't want to hit the kids. With the rows of blue booths lining the area, I don't have room to go sideways. The kids duck when I step over them. When I clear them, I breathe a sigh of relief. And run into the concession counter hard enough to knock a stack of cups to the floor.

CHAPTER FIFTEEN

TWAIN

I'm so impressed with the way Mabry stepped over Bryson and the little girl on the floor that it takes me a second to realize she just crashed into the counter. Kelsea's on it immediately, checking on the kids and Mabry first, before worrying about cleaning up any mess. Mabry's embarrassed by the scene, but she doesn't seem to be hurt. Bryson and Ryle are in awe of her quick move to dodge running over anyone, as boys would be. The little girl isn't hurt, but she's crying because her ice cream is now all over the floor.

Once Kelsea makes sure everyone is okay, she hurries back to the counter to get another cup of ice cream for the little girl.

"You guys go on," I tell Mabry and Truman. The kids are back on their feet now. Mabry's scrambling around to pick up the cups. "I'll get it, Mabry. You get back to Avery's party."

"I'm so sorry," she says—her voice half laughter and half sob. Her cheeks are still pink, but she's smiling. "I didn't mean to make you work after you're done for the day."

I feel Truman's eyes on me, but I don't have time to deal with that now.

"No problem," I tell Mabry. "Seriously. I'll take care of this. You go on back. Meet you there in a few minutes."

She eyes me wearily for a moment and finally agrees. She reaches for Bryson and Ryle, and when both take her hand, they move cautiously toward the door to the back rooms.

"What was that about?" Truman asks me.

"Get the cups, will you?" I don't even look at him. "I'll clean up the ice cream."

I feel his eyes on me as I leave him standing. I'm in for questions when this is done. But I don't have time for it now. I need to get the mess cleaned up before anyone skates through the ice cream.

When I come back from the storeroom with a mop and bucket, Truman has picked up the cups. He takes the caution: wet floor sign from me and waits while I mop up the spill. It takes all of two minutes, and then he follows me back to the storeroom.

"Seriously?" He blocks the door so I can't get by him.

"Seriously?" I throw it back at him and gesture for him to get out of my way.

"She doesn't know you own the place?"

I groan and throw my hands up in disbelief.

"Do we have to do this now?"

"What does she think you are? The janitor?"

"I don't know." I shrug. If anything, I'd rather she think I'm the groundskeeper, but I don't care to debate this with Truman.

"And you don't think keeping this from her is a bad idea?"

"I'm gonna tell her."

"When?"

"I don't know, Truman." I stack my hands on top of my head.

"Twain, it's a bad idea to start a relationship with a lie."

"It's not a lie," I mumble. "It's just a half truth. And we've only been out once."

"She's into you." Truman tips his head. His words are a firecracker in my gut. I want to ask what she said to make him say that, but I don't.

"Are we done?" I can't hide my irritation.

"This is because of Becca, isn't it?"

"What?"

"You don't wanna tell Mabry you own the place because your ex was a gold digger, and she burned you when she walked out."

Even though he's right, I have the urge to throw something back at him. Remind him that the only real relationship he's ever been in—the one that resulted in Ryle—is over, and he doesn't seem to have moved on as far as being lucky in love.

"I'll handle it." I grind the words out through clenched teeth.

"'kay." He nods and holds his hands up in surrender. "Whatever you say."

The smug look on his face makes me want to prolong the argument now. In fact, it's irrational, but there's a big part of me that wants to pop him and knock the grin from his face. He doesn't step out of my way, just turns sideways so I can slip out of the room.

The birthday party is in full swing when I find them in the second room on the right. Mabry's niece wears a cardboard crown, and Bryson and Ryle sit at the very end of the long table, legs dangling, skates flying back and forth. Barrie and Mabry are filling hot pink paper cups with lemonade. A guy I assume is Mabry's brother-in-law is putting candles on a cake.

When Mabry sees me, a sheepish grin crosses her face. I offer her a smile, wishing I could kiss her now. I wonder if her lips taste differently when she's embarrassed. If her kiss would be different. Softer. More reserved.

"Jules called."

I look over my shoulder when I hear Truman.

"I'm gonna take Ryle home later. Told her he was having cake and ice cream with your girlfriend. That okay?"

That irritation rolls over me again, but I nod.

"Yep."

"How'd you meet her?"

"Here." I lean back on the wall and fold my arms over my chest.

"And she doesn't know you own the place?"

"Nope."

"She knows your name, though?"

I turn my head and give Truman a silent store.

"Twain Woolff?" he says. "She knows you're a Woolff?"

"She does have my last name. I don't make a habit of asking women out without making sure they know who I am."

"And she still doesn't get it?"

"She lived here when she was younger. Moved away. Went to school. She wasn't around when I took over and started making changes to the park."

"Do you trust her?"

"Shut up."

This isn't the time for this conversation. We're speaking quietly, and a room full of ten-year-old girls is very noisy. But still, I don't want to stand here and debate this with Truman. I want to trust Mabry, but the simple truth is we haven't known each other long. While I don't intend to hide the fact that my family is ridiculously wealthy forever, it feels too soon to share it.

Truman and I sing with everyone to the birthday girl, and then Mabry's sister cuts the cake. The girls are still giggling and squealing at each other. Truman and I are used to the noise. Hattie and her friends could give these girls a run for their money. Bryson and Ryle do their fair share of giggling, heads together, yakking away while they destroy their cake. Ryle's big, sloppy smile makes me so happy it almost hurts.

"It's cool. Right?" Truman nudges me. Not sure what he's talking about, I glance at him. Ready to argue about Mabry again. Or ready to agree it's cool and let it go. Even if I'm frustrated with him, I know he's only harping on it because he's concerned. But when I look at him, his eyes are on Ryle. I nod and tell him yeah, it's cool.

CHAPTER SIXTEEN

Mabry

"Looked like Avery had a good birthday."

I put the last stack of Avery's presents in the back of Barrie and Will's SUV and look at Twain as I close the hatch.

"I think Barrie and Will might need a bigger house."

Twain laughs softly. "She reminds me of my niece." We walk back toward the rink where Barrie and Will are waiting with Avery's guests for their parents to pick them up. Twain links his fingers with mine. When I glance at him, he arches an eyebrow as if asking if it's okay. Maybe he thinks I haven't told Barrie we went out.

I did tell her. And I did tell her there were goodnight kisses, but there were no details shared. Those days mostly ended when Barrie and Will got married, although now and then, we overshare. When that happens, it's usually because we've had too much to drink.

I squeeze his fingers lightly, the buzz of anticipation making me feel light and dizzy, like I'm two drinks in. Only better.

"Thanks."

"For what?" I look at him with a frown.

We're at the door of the rink now, but neither of us moves to go inside. It's nice out here; definitely quieter. When we came outside, they were playing "The Cupid Shuffle" and there were seven ten-year-old girls clapping their hands and stomping and singing along in the vestibule of the building.

"Letting Ryle hang out with Bryson."

We walk on by the rink, heading nowhere in particular but in the general direction of the go-kart track. It's after five, but it's still warm enough that I'm uncomfortable in my jeans.

"Please." I roll my eyes. "Bryson loves him."

Twain's genuine smile melts my heart.

"Besides, he ate a tiny piece of cake—"

"He mauled a tiny piece of cake and ate the icing."

He did, although I'm not sure how much icing he ate versus how much he wore.

"So did Bryson." I shrug. "And Truman thanked me."

The mention of his brother draws a grumpy harrumph from Twain. He leans on the fence around the track. When he looks at me, he seems distracted.

"Ryle is a very quiet kid," he says softly. "Like, we're all kind of worried about him."

"How so?" I tip my head, sincerely curious and concerned.

"When he was little, Jules and Truman worried he was nonverbal. He just didn't talk."

"He was a chatterbox in there with Bryson," I remind him.

Twain nods his agreement. "He was. But when he's with us, me or my parents or even Truman and Jules, he's very quiet. It's interesting to see him interact with your nephew."

"Is Jules Truman's wife?"

"No." Twain straightens from the fence and starts walking again. I move with him, just because I want to be close to him. But also because I want to know more about his family. "They were together in college. She was pregnant when they broke up. They share custody of him."

"Oh." That surprises me, but I don't know why. Families come in all shapes and sizes now.

"I think that's been hard on Ryle," Twain mumbles.

"Maybe." I nod, but I'm frowning, thinking about the boy. "Did they have him tested?"

"Yeah. When he was three, they ran him through a battery of tests. Took him to a speech pathologist." He grins at me when he says this. "He tested very high in comprehension. And he did speak some to the pathologist. But he doesn't talk much around adults."

"Might be emotional trauma."

Twain glances at me and looks away.

"I'm not suggesting Truman and his ex are abusive. Just that maybe he feels tension between them. Or maybe tension between his mother and all of you."

"Maybe." Twain nods his head side to side. "We love Jules. All of us, but Truman, I guess. But yeah, I guess just having two lives, two homes like he does, swapping parents every other week or weekend might have some kind of effect on him."

"Truman seems like a good guy."

Twain grunts something that sounds heavy with frustration, but when he looks at me, he smiles and shrugs.

"He is," he says begrudgingly. "I have no idea what happened with him and Jules. Not sure anyone does. But as far as Ryle goes, he's a good dad."

That makes me smile. I haven't been around Ryle much but he's a cute kid, and don't we all want all kids to have parents who love them? Also, though, it makes me wonder what Twain would be like as a dad. He seems like a good uncle, so it seems to follow he'd be good with kids of his own.

We haven't talked about everything we want from our futures. But he did say that his ex didn't want kids. So, it seems logical to assume he does. We're still wandering the grounds. I could walk around like this with him all night. There's a light breeze, and the air smells fresh and sweet. I'm thinking about kissing him again when Jaws trots out of the line of trees at the far end of the property. He's got something in his mouth, but it doesn't look like a bird this time.

"Jaws!" Twain groans. He puts his fingers in his mouth and whistles. The dog's ears perk, and he runs to Twain immediately. "What now?"

The dog drops an old boot at Twain's feet.

"Really?" Twain leans over to pick it up and study it.

"Think someone's missing a shoe?"

"It's mine," he says with a sigh.

Curious where Jaws found Twain's boot—can he open a truck door with his snout?—I look around. Before I can ask, my phone buzzes in my back pocket. I slide it out and glance at the lot in front of the rink. Barrie waves at me from beside her SUV.

"Looks like my ride is leaving," I tell him.

Twain nods and starts walking that way.

"Now that you've had the experience of a birthday party at Wolverine Park, are you going to have yours here?"

I laugh softly as he links his fingers with mine again.

"It was fun."

"When is your birthday?"

"Two weeks."

"Will I see you before then?"

"I hope so."

We stop at the edge of the lot and turn to each other.

"I'm golfing with Truman and my dad tomorrow," he tells me. "But maybe we could do dinner tomorrow night?"

"Sounds good."

"I'll call you when we're done?"

"Looking forward to it."

He kisses me, but it's a quick, soft peck on my lips. Probably because my sister is standing there watching us like we're the leads in a romantic movie. I walk on air to Barrie's SUV thinking I *feel* like the lead in a romantic movie. It's free and easy and fun.

I like it. I hope there's more.

CHAPTER SEVENTEEN

Twain

I knew Truman wouldn't be able to keep his mouth shut, but I didn't think he'd be blabbing about Mabry before Dad ever teed off on the first hole. But here he goes, talking about roller skating yesterday and Ryle doing the Hokey Pokey with Mabry. Except he doesn't say Mabry; he says *Twain's girlfriend*. Which, of course, gets Dad's attention as he's squaring up for a practice swing.

I almost wish Dad would accidentally tap his ball off the tee when he does a little stutter swing and turns to look first at Truman and then me. Then he could focus on being mad at Truman instead of being curious about Mabry.

He doesn't, though. Instead, he puts the head of his driver on the ground and aims a mean *dad look* at me.

"He better not be talking about Becca."

As if I'm not even here, Truman snorts and answers, "Dad, really? You think Becca would be roller skating, let alone be doing the Hokey Pokey with Ryle?"

Dad reluctantly takes his eyes off my face and looks at Truman.

"Good point,' he agrees. "Who is she?"

He's still looking at Truman.

"Why am I here?" I ask them. "No one's teed off yet, and it's obvious you don't need me to talk about me."

"Who is she?" Dad swings his gaze back to me.

"Her name's Mabry," I hedge.

"Mabry?" He tips his head curiously, but there's a smile playing at his mouth.

"Family name," I explain.

"What does she do?"

"She's a speech pathologist at the hospital. I think she works with stroke and brain injury patients, mostly."

Apparently impressed, Dad raises his eyebrows and nods.

"And she roller skates?" He turns his back to me and looks at his ball again. "I like her already."

Truman and I exchange a glance, wondering if Dad's going to launch into the story about making a fool of himself on skates to get Mom's attention. Instead, he takes another practice swing and then steps up and drives the ball straight down the fairway.

"You like her, Truman?"

And here we go back to the two of them talking around me, about me.

"Yeah." Truman nods when Dad glances at him. He waves me on to drive next. I walk to the tee boxes, feeling like I have a big red x on my back. "I do. She's nothing like Becca."

"Tell me that's not the only thing you like about her." I tee up and then straighten and turn to look at them.

"It's not, but it kind of is," Truman mumbles with a shrug. "She's fun. Nice. She spent a Saturday afternoon with a bunch of ten-year-old girls and two little boys. She laughed with them and made goofy faces at the boys while they sang to her niece."

Truman looks at me. "That's what I like about her. And that woman is nothing like Becca."

He's got a point, but it sounds different when he explains it to my dad that way.

"She's good people," Dad says firmly. He gives me a nod as if granting his approval to date her. "How long's he been seeing her?"

Since he directed the question to Truman, I take a practice swing and then step closer and drive the ball. Not quite as straight as Dad, but it's not a bad shot.

When I pull my tee from the ground and turn back to them, they're still talking about me and Mabry.

"I don't know," Truman says to Dad. "But she doesn't have any idea who he is."

Irritated with Truman, I clench my teeth and drop my head back to stare at the perfect blue sky. Usually, being on the course at this hour is relaxing. Leave it to Truman to screw that up. Truman moseys over to the tee box, so lucky me, I get Dad's full attention.

"She doesn't know who you are?" he asks with a frown.

"She knows my name. But she's been gone from Basset for a long time. When she lived here, she was a kid. So, no, she doesn't know I own the park."

"She doesn't know you're a Woolff of Woolff Enterprises?"

"No. It's not like we're celebrities. We have money, but we don't grace movie screens."

"Son, she deserves to know the truth. You can't withhold that from her, just because that last little conniver burned you."

Truman takes his practice swings, and I daydream about throwing my club at him. At the very least, yelling at him as he takes his real swing just to throw him off. It would be a dick move, but at the moment, I don't care. I'm not one prone to headaches, but my frustration with my brother is pounding at the base of my neck, and it's not even eight a.m.

"I'm aware of that, Dad." My voice is calm. We're not a family to fight and hold grudges, which isn't to say we don't argue belligerently at times. Still, the golf course isn't the best place to hash this out.

"You that afraid of what she'll do when she finds out you've got money?"

Truman shanks the ball off the tee, and it snakes through the grass like an infield grounder. I choke back a laugh as he leans over and swipes at the tee, muttering with frustration when he sees it's broken. Truman makes his way back to our cart and slams his driver in his bag. He shoots me a look that dares me to say something, but I don't.

"I haven't known her that long, Dad." I slide into the driver's side as Dad claims the passenger seat in the golf cart. I release the brake and leave Truman to follow behind on us on foot. After all, he doesn't have far to go for his shot.

"Hey!" he hollers. "I need a club, jack."

Dad elbows me, so I stop. Truman trots up behind us and fishes a wood out of his bag.

"Nope." Dad grunts at him, so Truman chooses his four iron. I zip the car over to the side of the fairway and wait for Truman to hit again.

"How'd you meet her?" Dad turns to me for a second, but he's quick to look back at Truman.

"She was at the rink," I mumble with a shrug. "With her sister and nephew and his friend. It was...I dunno. A couple weeks ago. We talked. She's cute. Funny. She ended up showing up again the following week with her niece and nephew at the go-karts."

"You really like her."

"I do," I agree. "But is that a reason to go charging in like the world's on fire?"

"Maybe," Dad answers. "If she's that much of a catch, she might not be on the market long, son. If she feels the same about you, you better scoop her up before she gets away."

I hold my breath, waiting, knowing it's coming.

"You think your mother would have waited around for me to decide asking her out was the right thing to do?"

My eyes on Truman, I watch him swing. His ball flies and drops just on the edge of the green. Not a bad shot, but he'll bellyache about it. I nod when Dad continues talking about how Mom was such a looker and he had to take his chance to get her attention.

"I think you would like her," I tell Dad, just to shut him up. I love my parents' love story. But not when it's part of a lecture on something or other I should or shouldn't be doing.

"When do we get to meet her?" Dad asks me. I take off again and slow when the cart is even with my ball. "Does Mom know you're seeing her?"

"Nope."

"Well?" Dad gets out of the cart and looks at me as he reaches for his pitching wedge. "When do we get to meet her?"

"I don't know, Dad. You're a little intense."

"I promise not to ask her for grandchildren the first time I meet her."

"Go." I roll my eyes as Dad walks on to find his ball just short of the green.

"If Ryle likes her," Dad says with a shrug and then tips his head down to look for his ball.

Truman joins me at the cart as I find an iron.

"If you shoot better than me, you owe me a drink," Truman grumbles as he slides onto the driver's side of the cart.

"You're lucky I haven't wrapped a club around your neck." I narrow my eyes at him. "I don't need lectures while I'm golfing."

"That girl did things to your face I've never seen before, Twain." Truman slumps in the seat and folds his arms over his chest. "She makes you happy. I don't get why you don't snatch that up and run."

CHAPTER EIGHTEEN

MABRY

Twain's house is on the back edge of the property out at
Wolverine Park. When he called earlier, he suggested
grilling something for dinner. I thought it sounded nice,
relaxing, so he told me where to find him and I drove out.

The house is old, but most of it appears remodeled and or
redecorated. The hardwood floors look new, and the
walls are all a slate gray that I can't imagine are original to
the house. Big windows give the whole house an open
feeling, and the white cabinets in the kitchen make the
room feel bright and happy.

The counters are almost an apple green granite. Not
what I would have expected Twain's kitchen to look like,
but it's inviting and cozy. It smells like someone's been
baking all day. Twain catches me sniffing the air when he
turns from the refrigerator to offer me a beer.

"Are you burning a candle?" I ask him as I take the beer and nod my thanks.

"No." The smirk on his face is ornery. "I made brownies."

"You made brownies?"

"It's not hard, Mabry." He tips his own beer up for a swallow. "Open a box. Follow the instructions."

I laugh softly and shrug. "Still. They smell delicious."

"Let's go outside," he suggests.

We carry our bottles outside and sit at a nice patio table with a fire pit in the center.

"I love this!" I lean over the table to study the fake rocks that I assume glow when the fire pit is on. "Barrie and Will looked at one, but they ended up with something else."

"Where do they live?" he asks me.

"On the north end of Basset. Carver Street."

"So, close to you, then."

"It's not far," I agree.

It's beautiful out here. I don't know how much of the surrounding area is part of the land the house is on and how much is wild. But the lawn itself is immaculate. Like the grounds up by the park attractions the grass is thick and neatly trimmed. I wonder if Twain rents this place or if he owns it. Whatever the case, it's got to be convenient for him with work.

"How was the golf outing?"

Twain chuckles. "Do you play?"

Jaws comes tearing out the woods behind the house. His frenzied bark makes me jump, but Twain doesn't seem to hear him. Within seconds, the dog bounds back into the trees. I wonder if he's playing with another animal or something.

"I have played." I look back at Twain. "A few times. I don't play well. I would never claim to be a golfer."

"We should go sometime." He stretches his legs out in front of him and crosses his feet. He's wearing shorts again, and those muscled calves are within reach if I wanted to reach down and touch them. They're khaki, but the pockets are different than the ones he wore the night we had ice cream. He wears a t-shirt from a bar somewhere in Georgia, which makes me wonder where he's traveled and if there's somewhere he's always wanted to see.

"Golfing." I tip my head at him. "We should go golfing?"

He nods. It crosses my mind that though I am usually steady on my feet, I don't seem to be so surefooted around him. I imagine myself stepping in a hole and breaking an ankle on the golf course. That or losing control of the golf cart and taking out the flag on the first hole.

"I suppose if you need some entertainment."

His grin shoots electricity through my veins. Okay, so I would totally golf with him. I know he would beat me, and I am competitive, but it would be fun.

"My brother is a pain," he tells me.

"Truman?" I ask with a laugh. "I liked him."

"We didn't even tee off on the first hole before he told Dad I was seeing you."

I take a big drink of my beer. "Is that a bad thing?"

"Not at all." He shrugs. "I'd love for you to meet the rest of my family. But I can do without Truman being in a pain."

Sounds kind of familiar. I overheard Barrie talking to Mom about my new boyfriend.

"Dad shot a seventy." He puts his bottle on the table and stands. "I shot a seventy-six. And Truman shot an eighty."

"Uh-oh." I arch my eyebrows, wondering if his brother is a good sport. Twain just laughs.

"Be right back."

When he goes inside, I relax in my chair and study the tree line where Jaws has disappeared again. I bet this view is gorgeous in the fall. I like the little house I rent, but I'd love to be in a spot like this.

"Ribeyes okay?" he asks as he comes back outside.

"Perfect." I nod.

"So, Dad and Truman golf a lot." He talks as he gets the grill going on the opposite side of the deck. "For business. They're both good. I don't go often, but I'm not bad. Makes Truman nuts when I shoot better than he does." Twain looks at me and grins. "Which is exactly why I go."

"Your poor mother."

Twain barks a hearty laugh, but he nods. "Oh yeah. Mom had her hands full with us. And Harper was no angel, either."

"What do they do?"

"They're all in real estate."

Once he's satisfied that the gas is on and the grill is heating, he joins me at the table again. No wonder Twain works out here if his family is into real estate. Even if they have their own brokerage, I'd rather be outdoors like he is, doing what he does, than showing houses and sitting around a boardroom table talking appraisals and loans and titles.

"Your mom?" I ask him.

"She was. She's a full-time grandma now. Totally embraced that role."

"My mom loves being a grandma."

"Do your parents live here in town?"

"They're still in Springfield. But it's not a long drive, so they see Avery and Bryson a lot. Probably not as much as Mom would like."

"Do they have plans to come back here?"

I consider Twain's question. With an apologetic grin, I answer him.

"Well. If I settle down here. And end up having a family, I could see them moving back here. Dad's still working, but he could retire if he wanted to."

Twain leans forward, intense eyes pinning me in place.

"And do you plan to do that?"

I hold my breath for a second. Is he asking if I plan to have a family?

"Settle down here?"

"I like it here," I answer. "I love my job. I like being close to Barrie and Will and the kids. My grandma lives here, too. She was diagnosed with cancer recently. Kind of one of the major reasons I decided to move back."

Twain nods but he still watches me expectantly.

"And..." I arch an eyebrow. My cheeks are tingling, so I know I'm blushing to some degree. "There's a guy I've been seeing."

"Yeah?" He grins and quirks an eyebrow at me. "Does he play into reasons you might stick around here for a while?"

He reaches for me; his fingers cup my face, and he stares at me, his grin toned down to a sweet smile

"He does."

"I'm happy to hear that," he says quietly. His lips are warm when they touch mine, and when he deepens the kiss, I taste the beer on his mouth. Jaws tears up out of the trees again, but this time he trots up the steps to join us on the deck. "I swear this dog is like a little kid. Always sticking his nose in the middle of things."

When Twain ends the kiss, he stands and goes back inside. Jaws turns his full attention to me and stares at me with baleful eyes.

"You like being in the middle of things, don't you?" I hold my hand out to him, pleased when he moves closer and parks beside my chair. When I scratch his ears, he rests his head on my lap.

"Harper said Ethan can't quit talking about Bryson," Twain announces when he returns with a plate.

"That's cute." I watch him use tongs to toss two big steaks on the grill as I absently stroke Jaws' nose.

"I can't get over the way Ryle took to him." Twain shakes his head. Satisfied with the steaks, he closes the grill and joins me again.

"You're so lucky to live out here." Relaxing again in my chair, I look around. Clouds like cotton hang low over the trees behind us. They're so white, they look scribbled in with crayon on the perfect blue backdrop of sky.

"You think so?" He sounds surprised.

"I bet it's gorgeous in the fall."

"It is." His voice sounds a bit gruff, but when I glance at him, he offers me that laid back smile. "I hope you'll be here with me to see it."

His words wrap around me and warm me. Again, I'm struck by how comfortable I feel with him. I'm attracted to him, and with every kiss we share, I want more. And I know he does, too. But on the other hand, being with him here, now, watching a summer breeze rustle the leaves out behind the house is perfect.

I'm content to be with him like this like I've never felt before with anyone I've dated. And if anything, it feels like this connection we have out here in the real world will enhance the intimacy between us when we make love.

He reaches for my hand, and we watch our fingers link.

Okay, all that being true, his touch makes me a little feverish. I like that we're not rushing to the good stuff. It makes me feel like the good stuff will be here to stay when it finally happens. But on the other hand, I need to acknowledge where we're going. And I need him to do the same.

"So." He rubs his thumb over the back of my hand. "Your birthday."

I laugh nervously and wait for him to continue.

"I think you should roller skate. And I think probably your sister and her husband would come to your party. And I think I would come. And probably Truman. Harper and her husband."

"You wanna throw me a skating party for my birthday? With your family?"

"That's not even the good part." His voice is gruff again, and it hits me that it's longing. Lust. Sex. Whatever you want to call it. We're sitting out here enjoying each other and the evening and thinking the same thing.

"What's the good part?" I ask him with a sly grin.

"You could stay over," he says softly. I watch for the twinkle in his eyes, feeling a rush of heat when I see it. "If you want."

"I do," I say instantly.

"Okay." He stands, abruptly breaking the moment. "That's settled." His grin is wicked as he crosses the deck to check the steaks.

"What's settled?"

Jaws nudges me with his nose as if to remind me he's still there and would like another scratch.

"I'm planning your birthday party."

CHAPTER NINETEEN

Twain

Mabry looks incredible tonight. She's wearing dark wash denim with a black sleeveless blouse. When I saw her walk in, she was wearing black heels, but now she's rocking the fashionable patchwork roller skates. She's taken more time with her hair tonight, left it down and it hangs in loose curls over her shoulders. Dark eyeliner and shimmery shadow makes her eyes pop.

"Happy birthday."

She turns to me smoothly, graceful on the skates, and gives me that smile I've already come to love.

"Hey!"

I'm all in when she reaches for me, cups the back of my head, and draws me in for a kiss.

"Thanks." She loops her arms around my shoulders and

turns back to look at me with a sweet smile. "This is great. I'm so excited for tonight."

"Good." I nod as I slide my arms around her waist. I'm totally aware of my siblings watching us, of her sister and brother-in-law standing here, watching us expectantly. At least my parents aren't here. They're watching all the grandkids, who are miffed that they were not invited to the party I'm having for Mabry. I promised them earlier we would go skating over the weekend, and I would ask Mabry to come along. But I assume at some point, this party will end up over at the casino, and the kids can't be there.

"Are you totally mine for the night?" She quirks a brow at me, her lips tipped up in a smirk.

"All yours."

"Off the clock?" She draws back further to look me up and down. Her nod and smile indicate that she approves of my jeans and black button-down shirt. It's rare for me to announce I am totally off the clock, but I've told my employees I'm on personal time tonight, that this party is for someone special.

"All yours," I repeat. She throws her head back to whoop it up and then hugs me tight, like she can't get close enough.

"Twain Woolff!" Harper's voice cuts through the Post Malone song playing. With a laugh, I ease away from Mabry and spin her around, my arm still around her shoulders.

"Harp, this is Mabry Aliston."

My sister is all smiles as she skates over to us, arms outstretched toward Mabry.

"Mabry, my sister, Harper and her husband, Keith."

"Hey!" Harper stops just short of mauling Mabry. She makes an enthusiastic grab for Mabry's hands and blasts her with a big smile. "I'm so excited to meet you!"

"Hi, Harper!" Mabry sounds just as excited as my sister.

"God, you're gorgeous." Harper lets go of Mabry's hands to play with her hair. "I love your hair."

Mabry's laugh is sweet. I haven't seen this side of her; she's like a teen at her sweet sixteen party. I wonder how much of her excitement is anticipation about later tonight, if she still plans to stay over.

"Oh my God!" Mabry squeals when Cliffie starts "Ladies Night." She glances at her sister, and suddenly, she and Harper skate off together, grabbing Barrie's hand as they go.

"I love her." Truman shrugs. "If you don't put on a ring on that, I will."

"Shut up."

"You skating?" Truman asks me.

"You think I'm gonna let her skate with other jerks with skates?" I tip my head to look down at Truman's feet. He's not wearing skates yet.

Truman snickers.

"You skating?" I look at Mabry's brother-in-law.

He makes a show of looking at his feet, and then scoots off toward the rink.

"I need a size ten." Truman smacks me in the gut.

"Dude, get your own skates."

"Ryle is seriously mad at you." Truman follows me to the skate rental counter.

"That your girl?" Cliffie nearly dives over the counter, grinning ear to ear.

"That's Mabry," I tell him.

"That's so cool."

Cliffie started working for me after Becca left, so he's never known me to have any interest in women, other than the general way men find women attractive.

"Well, if he's gonna be stupid about it, he might lose her," Truman tells Cliffie. My employee grins at my brother and shakes his head.

"Nah. The boss has got this one," he says.

While they're talking about women—Truman's rattling about some girl he met in Miami—I slip behind the counter to grab skates. I find the ugliest pair of size tens possible and set them on the counter for Truman. I hear him griping about them as I slip into the office and find my speed skates.

"Nice." Truman joins me in the office. I laugh at him, but I don't bother looking up at him as I quickly put the black and white skates on. "These are hideous."

"Quit bellyaching." I glance his way as I stand. I tuck my casual tan loafers aside and offer my brother a big grin as I skate out and leave him sitting there.

"Ladies Night" is done, and now some Walk the Moon song is playing. The girls are still on the floor, so I stand for a moment and watch them. Mabry is beautiful, and it's not even her pretty curls and made-up eyes that makes my blood pump harder. It's her carefree style, her ease and her confidence. And the fact that she radiates happiness.

Dad's right.

It's early for us, but I need to make sure she knows I want her. I want everything about her.

"Twain!" She sees me watching her and waves and then turns it into a motion to join her. Barrie and Will are a few feet behind them, but Harper and Keith skate with her. In fact, it looks like Harper is talking at her as they glide over the floor.

"Give her a break, Harp!" I lean close and holler as I skate past my sister. "I'm sorry. My siblings don't know how to behave." I grab Mabry by the waist, but we keep moving smoothly.

"This is great, Twain!" Mabry leans into me for a second. "Thank you for doing this!"

"You are beautiful." I kiss the top of her head before she straightens up and puts a sliver of space between us. She flashes me a big smile.

"So are you," she says. She gets close to me again as we navigate the turn at the end of the rink and head back the other way. She reaches for me and takes my hand. "I don't know what it is with you, Twain, but it just feels right."

For me too, but before I can say that, Cliffie's voice cuts in and announces that we have a special birthday girl at the rink. Mabry looks at me with big eyes, but I shrug. Cliffie's not doing my bidding up there. Wouldn't surprise me if Truman put him up to that, but then again, Cliffie thinks Mabry's cool.

I drop my head back and laugh when the next song starts. Mabry looks at me curiously.

"I like country music," I tell her.

"I love this song," she says so softly, I almost miss it. "So, I guess you probably have an in here for requests, huh?"

"You could say that." I move in front of her and turn easily to skate backwards. Mabry grins as I slip my arms around her waist. "Why? Something you wanna hear?"

"Well, this is nice." She meets my eyes.

"Still planning to stay over?" I ask her, hoping I don't look as pathetic as that sounded to my ears.

"Mmm. I brought an overnight bag." She tips her head.

"Good. I can't wait to get you alone."

"Me too." She nods.

Aware that we can't fall too far into each other's eyes right now, I give myself a mental shake. "What do you want to hear? I'll hit Cliffie up."

She grins. "I had a skating party when I turned eight."

"I bet you were cute."

"I was so cute." She laughs. "All glasses and freckles. But I was the top scorer on my soccer team, and I hit three home runs that year."

"We still need to go golfing." I would love to see her in motion. She's so smooth on skates; she has to be a sight in sports she enjoys.

"I wanna hear some eighties stuff."

We hold the eye contact a moment longer. "On it."

CHAPTER TWENTY

MABRY

This might be the best birthday I've had since I turned eleven when my parents took me and Barrie to Disneyworld. Before tonight, I saw Twain as laid back and easy going. While that's still there, he cuts loose tonight, and we're skating and laughing and singing. I can tell Barrie and Will like him, and I'm as comfortable with his siblings as I am with him.

Is this what it feels like? I think I've been in love before—that kind of love you grow through to get to the real, forever thing. But is this what the forever kind of love starts like? Feeling like he's the missing part of me? Like we're two halves of the same whole?

There's hardly a minute that we're not touching all through the night. When we skate, we hold hands. When we're playing air hockey against Barrie and Will or any combination of his siblings, we're constantly high-fiving.

When we're in the concession area, he's got his arm around my shoulders, and I'm resting my head on his chest.

True to his word, he put a request in with Cliffie, and we've skated to everything from "Funkytown" to "Another One Bites the Dust." I told Barrie I don't want gifts, but she and Will give me a gift certificate for a spa day, and Barrie gives me a cute blouse with matching earrings. Harper and Keith give me a gift card to Harvey's, which makes me wonder if Twain mentioned our date there. Truman, though, gives me a beautiful picture Ryle drew for me. It's a rainbow with some stick figures at the end by a pot of gold. In case I wasn't sure, Ryle has written my name with his and Bryson's.

I'm teasing Twain about it when we leave. We've traded our skates back for our shoes, and we're walking through the parking lot across the campus to the casino. I'm not a big gambler, but I'm happy to just be out with Twain and my sister and his family. We're going to grab a spot at the casino and maybe order some appetizers. Twain says the stuffed mushrooms and the candied Brussels sprouts are good. He would know, right?

The music in the casino makes me think of Vegas. That mindless trance beat. Barrie and I went to Vegas together a couple of years ago. We had a good time. Tonight is better. I liked Truman before, but I'm getting to know him better tonight. He's sharp with a dry sense of humor. Plus he's Ryle's dad, so that's like a hundred points right there.

"I think Twain's a keeper," Barrie says when we're standing together at a small round table. Harper and Keith are at a slot machine that shows a well-endowed woman falling out of a bikini top. Harper is feeding the machine quarters, and Keith is standing at her side, cheering her on. He's sipping on a pour of Knob Creek. At the table with us and Will, Truman and Twain are arguing Batman and Superman, and it feels like the kind of sibling argument that they pick up often, with no one gaining ground.

I meet Barrie's eyes with a smile.

"I like him a lot," I whisper to her.

She nods and gives me that stupid older sister smile, like she knows more than me about life. She's only two years older than me; the notion that she's well-versed and experienced in life while I'm not, frustrates me.

"I need to go to the bathroom," she tells me. I do, too so I follow her. Twain glances at me and nods, like he knows where we're going.

"Wait!" Harper calls as we pass her. "I gotta go too!" She jumps up from the padded stool she sits on and kisses Keith in the general area of his mouth. "Win big for me, baby."

Barrie and I laugh at her as the three of us make our way to the ladies' room.

"This place is great," I say as we burst into the room. Barrie grabs the first stall.

"Twain's got a good thing here." Harper says it as if in agreement as she ducks into her own stall. Confused, I stare at her closed door for a second before slipping into my own stall to take care of business.

"We should go to Vegas," Barrie announces a few moments later. I frown as I zip my jeans. Sounds like she's had enough to drink, but as far as I know, she's only had two beers.

"Vegas!" Harper agrees. "Oh my god! Yes! We should go to Vegas! Have you been?"

We all emerge from our stalls at the same time.

"A few times," Barrie tells Harper. "Mabry and I went a couple of years ago."

"Tell me you did Freemont!"

I slip between them to wash my hands.

"We did Freemont," I promise Harper.

"We ziplined!" Barrie tells her.

"Well, I'm jealous!" Harper says as we step out of the ladies' room. "Keith wouldn't let me. He said I was drunk!"

"Sounds like Will," Barrie agrees.

We move back through the casino, raised voices at a blackjack table drawing our attention as we pass. Two guys appear to be at a stand-off. The dealer says something, and then the tension seems to ease, and the guys sit down again.

The appetizers are there when we come back to the table. Twain and Truman are going at it now about the Blues and the Blackhawks, but it's good natured. When I slip up beside him and press into him, Twain turns to me with a grin and then picks up a Brussels Sprout and feeds it to me. I never thought of vegetables as sexy, but I'm so turned on, I want to officially end the party and head back to Twain's house.

Harper and Truman fall into a discussion about the best James Bond, and Twain and Will are talking about Metallica. I'm watching all of it, wondering how this feels so right when I've just moved back to Basset. I want this to be my life.

Twain stills, glass at his lips, when there's a loud crashing noise from a distance. He and Harper share a look, and then he glances at Truman.

"Twain!" A male voice calls as two guys hurry toward our table. One of them is dressed in black trousers and a black button-down shirt. I assume he's a dealer, since they're all dressed the same. The other one is in a suit and tie, but he looks hard and stern. When he stands at our table, eyes on Twain, I notice a gun tucked into a gun belt around his waist.

Security guard.

"What's going on?" Twain asks them. All traces of fun

are gone from his face now. His eyes are hard and serious, his mouth set in a grim line.

"Boss!" Another voice yells.

Twain looks that way, and then before the two guys at our table can speak, Twain rushes away, toward the blackjack table. Barrie looks at me like she thinks I can give her an explanation. I shrug and look to Harper.

"What's going on?" Harper asks the dealer standing with us. The other guy—the one I assume is a security guard—rushes away after Twain. "Do we need the police?"

"On the way," the guy tells her. "Two guys have been ripping at each other all night. Sounds like one of them owes the other some big money. Keeps dodging the pay back."

"Good idea to come out and gamble more," Harper mumbles.

"The guy who did the loaning decided to throw a punch. They're all over each other, and then a chair went flying. Ended up hitting a woman who happened to be walking by at the time."

"Is she hurt?"

The dealer shrugs. "Ambulance is coming. She's got a bump on her head, but she seems okay."

"Did the chair hit her in the head?" Harper yelps.

"No." The dealer finally looks around at the rest of us

and offers us a mumbled apology. "Hit her in the side, but she stumbled a bit. Hit her head on the wall."

"Well, this is just what Twain needs," Truman grumbles as he walks away in the general direction of the blackjack tables.

"Sorry to ruin your night." The guy looks right at me as he says this. "There's never any trouble here. The one night the boss man wants to be left alone, this crap goes down."

I feel Barrie and Will's eyes on me, but I don't look at either of them. The situation is becoming clearer, though not the way it should be. I think I just found out that Twain is the boss here, rather than the groundskeeper or jack-of-all-trades janitor. Maybe it's not a big deal, but then again, I feel like he should have told me himself.

"The press is going to jump on this." Truman shoots Harper a pointed look.

Harper sighs and nods. We hear the distant sounds of sirens approaching. Harper glances at Keith and then looks at me. Before I can say a word, Twain rushes back to our table. He reaches for me and settles his hand on my arm, but he looks at Harper.

"Do you want me to call Dad?" Harper asks him.

"Nope. I got it." He shakes his head and then turns to me. "Mabry, I'm so sorry. I have to deal with this."

"Okay." I nod. Of course, he needs to deal with this. If

he's the boss, it's his problem, no matter that it's my birthday.

"You can wait here, or you guys can all go to the house and wait for me."

"I'm fine," I promise him. He nods, gives Truman a look, and then rushes away again as a uniform cop yanks the front door open and strides in.

"Mr. Woolff?" The cop says to Twain.

"Yeah, this way." Twain leads the cop away from the main entrance. Most of the customers here have stopped to watch the action; some of them follow Twain and the cops, but now some go back to the slot machines and whatever else they were doing. I don't mind waiting for Twain, but the magic sparkle on my birthday has dulled.

"You wanna go hang out at Twain's?" Harper asks me.

I didn't want to when Twain mentioned it, but now that the cops are here, and I see Twain and the security guy walking two guys into an office with the cops behind them, I'm ready to leave.

"Sure."

Barrie hooks her arm around my neck and drags me a few steps away from our table.

"What's going on?"

I look up at her with a shrug. "How would I know?"

"I thought he was the groundskeeper, Mabry."

"I did, too."

"He's a Woolff." She says this like it should mean something to me. I nod, because of course I know his name is Woolff. I wouldn't go out with a guy if I didn't even know his full name. "You didn't tell me he was a Woolff."

"Why does it matter?" I tip my head and narrow my eyes at my sister.

"Woolff is the biggest money name in Basset these days." She shrugs and nods her head back at the table. "Your boyfriend's loaded."

"What?"

"His dad owns half the town. Owns a hotel and casino in Vegas. Has real estate investments all over the globe."

"How—what?" I give myself a mental shake and try again. "How do you know it's his dad?"

"Really?" Barrie rolls her eyes. "That guy called Twain the boss man. He owns this place, Mabry."

Her words shock me, but I try to hide it. I'm not sure what it means. I'm not sure it's a problem. But until I figure it out, I don't want my sister to see how confused I am by all of this.

"What if he does?" I ask her quietly.

Barrie tips her head back and groans, apparently frustrated with me now. "I don't know. It just seems like something he should have told you."

"Hey." Harper approaches us and touches my shoulder. "Are you okay?"

"Yeah, I'm fine."

"This has never happened before," Harper says to us. "Twain runs a tight ship."

"Does he own the place?" Barrie asks her.

Harper nods, but she bites her lip when Barrie gives me a sharp look. "He didn't tell you that?"

"Tell me what, exactly?" I ask Harper.

"He owns the park," she says quietly. "Wolverine Park."

"No."

"I'm sorry." Harper frowns. "I'm sure he planned to tell you."

I wonder. I mean, he was planning to *sleep* with me. You'd think maybe he might have planned to tell me at some point that he owned the whole complex—that he wasn't just the laidback groundskeeper I assumed him to be.

I'm not sure it matters. Or why it matters. But it bothers me. Here I've spent the evening thinking this is how it starts. That this feeling I have with Twain, this excitement at being with him, the thinking about him all the time, the pure perfection of just spending time with him is the beginning of forever. And I didn't know something so basic about him.

"It's okay." I shake my head, because even if it isn't okay, it's not Harper's problem. Or Barrie's. "I'll talk to him later. I'm sure he'll explain."

"Are you sure?" Barrie asks me. She smooths her hand over my back to comfort me as if I've just found out Twain's married, instead of the owner of Wolverine Park.

"Yeah. I'll just go hang out at his house. We'll talk."

Barrie nods. "Call me? If you need anything?"

"I will," I assure her. I would. If I needed anything. But I don't know what it would be or what Barrie could do about it. I just need to talk to Twain.

"I'll drive you to the house," Harper offers.

"I'd rather walk," I tell her. She starts to protest, but when I only stare at her, she nods. It's not quite dark, and I would hope the campus is safe for women to walk. And I need to be alone with my thoughts. Maybe Twain isn't in the same spot with me as I am with him. Maybe he's just passing time with me. Maybe this was just going to be a fling. Why trust someone you don't plan to keep around long?

CHAPTER TWENTY-ONE

Twain

It takes way longer than you would think it should to deal with the police and the guys who got in the fight in my casino. We have to fill out the police report. The cops arrest both for assault and battery. The EMTs deal first with the woman who was lucky enough to get hit by the chair one of them threw. She seemed fine; in fact, she insisted she was fine, but for insurance purposes and because of the police report, they took her to the ER to make sure she was okay. They patched up the black eyes and bloodied lips on the troublemakers. I stayed longer with the dealer at the table where it happened and my security guy, so we could write up the incident report for insurance.

By the time I walked out of the office with the intention of finding Mabry, my whole group was gone. I wasn't surprised, but it was still disappointing. The table where the fight broke out had been cleaned up, and business was back to usual. But Mabry was gone. I considered calling her but decided to walk home first and see if she might be waiting there for me.

I feel a weight lift off my shoulders when I get close enough to the house to see the golden glow of light in the front window. Someone's there. I have to assume it's her. When I step up on the porch, I hear Jaws's low, throaty bark from inside. He greets me when I push the front door open.

"Hey buddy." I lean over and cup his big face in my hands and rub his ears. Used to be, that face and his happy tail were all I needed to come home to. And then I met Mabry, and that quickly, I'm desperately hoping she's here. That tonight didn't ruin what we had going.

Jaws slips past me into the night. I watch him for a second and then let the screen door close. When I turn back, Mabry is sitting on the end of the sofa with her legs tucked up under her. She looks up from a book as she slips her finger inside it to hold the page. I look closer and see that it's *The Adventures of Huckleberry Finn*. She's pulled it from my shelf. For a moment, I feel light and hopeful. If she's holding her place, she must plan to come back and read more.

"Hey." My voice is gruff. I'm tired, and I know she's worn out and probably frustrated that her birthday ended this way. I just wonder what else she's thinking.

Our eyes meet. That thrill of hope I felt a second ago

vanishes when I see the grim set of her mouth and the cool look in eyes that are usually warm and inviting.

"I'm sorry that took me so long."

It hits me that we didn't finish our appetizers. As far as I know, Mabry didn't drop a quarter in a slot machine. I don't need her quarters, but I wanted her to enjoy herself tonight, and slot machines can be fun now and then.

She takes a deep breath and sets the book on the end table. I feel a pang when she loses her page.

I have a birthday cake in the kitchen. Nothing fancy; I made it for her because the idea of telling her I did it for her made me happy. I also have a bouquet of flowers for her—a colorful, summery mix—and a bottle of champagne. While I hoped she would stay over, while I've thought about making love to her every day since the first time I saw her, I was looking forward to a little private party before we took things upstairs.

I'm not sure she's interested now.

"Was anyone hurt?" she asks me as she stands.

I watch her long legs unfold and then jerk my gaze back up to meet hers.

"Um. The woman had a bump on her head. I think she was okay, but they took her to the ER to be sure. Both men are fine. Some cuts and bruises."

She nods. I wait, wondering if she's the sort of woman to go on the offensive when she's angry. If she'll yell or if she'll freeze me out with silence. She simply stares at me. She's not pleased, but she doesn't look ready to go for my throat, either.

"I made you..." I hesitate and then shrug. If she walks out of here because I made a stupid mistake by not trusting her, then maybe we weren't on the same page to begin with. Yes, it's obvious we have a physical attraction. Yes, I should have told her before she found out like this that I own Wolverine Park. But I don't think this is grounds for calling it quits on what we might have together. "I made you a cake."

Still, she only stares at me.

I clear my throat and take a few steps into the living room.

"And I have champagne."

To my relief, Mabry follows me into the kitchen. I glance at her as she sees the flowers and the cake. She's touched, which stirs up a mix of emotion in me. I want her to talk, to tell me what she's thinking, rather than storm out of here and never look back. On the other hand, I hate that my mistake hurt her.

"So." She licks her lips and folds her arms over chest as she lifts her gaze to meet mine. "We're doing this? We're going to have cake and champagne. For my birthday."

"I want to," I say with a nod. I won't push it, because as desperate as I am to keep her here, being melodramatic seems wrong. Fake. I know I screwed up. I just want the chance to apologize.

"Why didn't you tell me?" She presses her lips together. For a second, my mind is there on her mouth. Kissing her. Drinking champagne with her. Tasting the sweet alcohol on her lips.

"I'm sorry."

"Are you?"

"Mabry." I toss my hands up and spin around in the room, helpless to defend myself.

"Because it feels like you didn't trust me." She speaks quietly. "I packed a bag to spend the night with you tonight. Never mind that we haven't known each other long, it feels like we were made to be together."

Her words are a cold fist around my heart.

"At least it feels that way to me," she says with a shrug. "I've never felt so right, so perfectly matched with someone in my life. I had every intention of sleeping with you tonight, of falling in love with you, because as outrageous as that seems, I've already started."

"Mabry."

"And then some freak thing happens, and that's how I find out who you are? That you own Wolverine Park? That your dad is a real estate tycoon?"

"I was going to—"

"Do you know what that looks like to me?" she interrupts me. "And probably to my sister and her husband? It looks like we hung out a few times, and you invited me to stay at your place tonight for a crazy fling, and that tomorrow, you'll hand me my walking papers and I won't see you again."

"That's not true."

"Because why would you want to trust a fling with that kind of information?" she continues. "Except, my sister figured it out before I did. Because she's been back in Bassett longer. She recognized the name once we figured out you own the park. Your family obviously knows who you are. What you are."

She's right. I should have talked to her about this. I should have told her on our first date.

"You made a fool of me, Twain."

"What I am," I say and shake my head.

"What?"

"That's why I didn't tell you yet." I sigh and lift my arms to stack my hands on the top of my head. "The money doesn't define me. Maybe the park does. Because I like being outdoors. Because I like seeing families have fun. Because it's good for the community. But the money isn't me."

She raises her eyebrows.

"Most women I've dated see dollar signs instead of a man." He shrugs. "My ex always wanted more. She wanted me to be more. She hated that I chose work boots and khakis and fixer-upper over Armani suits and board rooms and international business."

Mabry flinches. "You didn't give me a chance to show you that I see you."

"I know you do," I say quietly. "I wasn't testing you. But you love being out here. You love my house. My dog. The grounds. You liked Harvey's, and you drink beer, and you like to roller skate. *Ryle* likes you."

"But you weren't testing me." She rolls her eyes.

"Yes, I should have told you, Mabry. That my family has big money. That I own the park. That I have no drive to own more. I'm never gonna be a boardroom kind of guy. This is who I am, right here. I should have told you why Becca left me."

She nods and brushes at her eyes.

"But you can't assume I wasn't going to tell you tonight."

"Twain."

"I wouldn't have asked you to sleep with me without telling you who I am. The rest of it. I know you don't want to believe that, but I'm asking you to anyway."

"Did you love her?"

"Becca?" I shrug. "I dunno. I wanted to. In the beginning." I lean on the counter at my back. "With you,

I didn't have to think about it. I didn't have to want anything with you. It was just there. Naturally."

She stares back at me silently.

"Like we were made for each other. Like I was here waiting my whole life for you to walk in and be home."

Mabry swallows hard and nods.

"What kind of cake is it?" she mumbles with a nod at the cake on the table.

"Chocolate."

Head tipped, she lifts her eyes to look at me.

"Are you going to sing to me?"

"I can," I offer, "but the better gift might be not singing to you."

She laughs softly and then shakes her head.

"Do you understand why I'm upset?"

"Yes."

She nods again.

"For what it's worth, I am sorry."

Mabry pulls out a chair and sits down. "I know."

"We could still have your birthday party."

I move quickly to get the champagne from the refrigerator. She watches me take the cage off and pop the cork.

"I can't sleep with you, Twain," she says as I pour the bubbly liquid into the flutes I put out on the table earlier.

Frustrated with myself, I nod and wonder what to say to that.

"I get it. But I hope we can be friends."

"Tonight."

Our eyes meet.

"What?" I put the bottle down and lean over to rest my hands on the table.

"Not tonight," she says again. "I'm not ready. But..."

She reaches over the table to rest her hand on mine. "I mean, I like Ryle. And according to him, you would have to tell me I'm pretty every day—"

"Yeah," I agree, "but you would have to make me coffee every morning."

A small smile plays at her lips. "I'll bring it. For now."

"Yeah?"

I turn my hand over and take hers. She stands as I move around the table.

"I'll bring you coffee for now," she says again. "Maybe someday I'll feel like making it for you."

I slide my arms around her waist and kiss her forehead.

"Fair enough."

"Anything else you need to tell me?" She smooths her hands up over my chest and rests them on my shoulders. "Do you own a yacht? Do you do annual safaris in Africa?"

"No and no." I shrug. "Do you want me to?"

"No." She kisses the corner of my mouth. "I just want you to be the man I met here at the skating rink."

"No one special."

"That man's all the special I need."

This time our kiss lasts a bit longer, and the only reason I break it is to hand her a flute. I want her to drink, so I can taste the champagne on her lips. I'll bet the park it's the best champagne I'll ever taste.

THE END

Thank you for reading Twain and Mabry's story. Please consider leaving a review on Amazon, Goodreads, or other bookish websites.

Keep reading for a peek at Truman and Julie's story.
RINGS ON WINGS

RINGS ON WINGS

Chapter 1

Julie

"Jules? Did you hear me?"

I blink at my friend Dani and finally pull it together enough to nod. I even manage to smile.

"Yeah, Dani!" Of course, I'm excited for Dani and Eric. They're having a baby. It's their first. What's not to be happy about? Dani and I have been friends since kindergarten. Best friends forever. *Besties!* I want Dani to have it all—perfect marriage, wonderful husband, and a baby. *A family.* She deserves it.

But for just a half a second there, Dani's news hurts.

Because once upon a time, I thought I was going to have the same thing. Truman Woolff and I were a thing for four years. From the time we were seniors in high school until we graduated from college—Truman and I were inseparable.

And then I got pregnant.

Sure, I was old enough to have sex. Old enough to be responsible for a baby. And I was happy about being pregnant. I read all the books I could find on pregnancy and parenting, and I went back and forth on baby names a hundred times before deciding what to name Ryle.

The only difference between Dani and me is that she and Eric are married.

But when I got pregnant, Truman and I split up.

"I'm so excited for you!" I gush, because that little pin prick of pain has passed, and the five years since then, the five years of me and Ryle, puff me up and make me happy. "When are you due? Do you know what you're having? Have you told anyone?"

Dani chuckles and stretches her legs out on her lounge chair. Eric is in their house getting burgers ready to put on the grill. Ryle is with Truman's parents, so I have the evening to myself. Funny how I always think I need a night to myself, but the second I leave Ryle with Truman or anyone in his family, I miss him.

I sip a canned margarita and close my eyes as I put it back down.

"We haven't told anyone yet, but our parents," Dani tells me. "And I don't know what it is."

"I love it," I say, eyes still closed. Now that the little wave of envy is gone, I'm excited to think of all the things my best friend is going to experience. Excited that I'll get to share in most of those things, because odds are, Ryle will be my only child.

"Eric's hoping for twins."

"You should definitely punish him for that." I turn my head on my lounge chair and peek at Dani. She grins. One baby is so much more work than I ever imagined. Then again, Dani has Eric, so things will be somewhat easier for her.

"Hey!" Dani lifts her foot and swings it my way to nudge my leg. She misses, but she has my attention, because I'm laughing at her now. "What did you think of Eric's cousin?"

"He was nice." I shrug and rest my eyes again.

"I think we're going to ask him to be the baby's godfather."

"Oh!" I blink and nod, excited all over again. "Yeah, Jerad seemed like a nice guy."

"And we would like you to be the baby's godmother."

I roll my eyes up to see Eric as he rounds our chairs on the way to the grill, a plate loaded with burgers in hand. He's watching me for my reaction to his announcement.

"Really?" I'm too keyed up now to sit still, so I lean

forward and when that's not close enough to Dani, I scooch forward some on my chair.

"Mm-hmm." Dani nods.

"I'm honored, Dani," I say sincerely. She has two sisters and five brothers; I totally assumed she would choose someone in her family to be the godmother to her baby. "I would love to stand for the baby."

"Good." She nods, and then Eric repeats her, his voice loud and firm.

Now that it's decided, I flop backwards again in the chair and take another drink.

"So." She clears her throat which is my first indication that she's up to something. Dani sucks at Poker. She could never win Old Maid when we were kids. And she was terrible when we played Clue. She can't bluster or fib; she gets all nervous. Same as now, when she's about to suggest something she knows I won't like.

"No."

"Hear me out."

"Nope."

"He's going to be in town this weekend." She ignores me. "And we thought we could all go out. Maybe get pizza or something."

Is she seriously trying to set me up with Eric's cousin Jerad? Because as nice as the guy is, there's no way I'd want to go out with him. He's cute—got a little cowlick on the back of his head, usually covers it with a ball cap. And he's got a sweet smile. Plays the trumpet in some band where he lives. Sings at his church. And he loves my friend like she's his sister.

But he's not Truman.

I know it's not fair, but since getting pregnant with Ryle and losing Truman, I compare every guy I meet to Truman. No one measures up.

I've dated. I've tried to move on. I spent seven months with a guy when Ryle was three. The guy adored Ryle, and after everything, that was the top priority on my list. I could have settled for him. He would have been good to me and Ryle. But he didn't deserve that. So, I broke it off with him before it got too complicated.

I still go out sometimes, most often with groups of friends from the bank where I work. And I do date occasionally, but I've resigned myself to the fact that it's not meant to be. I loved Truman Woolff so deeply, for so long, I don't have it in my heart to love another man.

At least Ryle has a relationship with Truman and his family.

"Jules, I just want you to be happy," Dani whines.

"I know." I turn my head to look at her again. "And I appreciate that. But remember. There're different roads to happiness, Dani. I've got Ryle. No one's ever going to take away my happy when I have Ryle."

"But you could—"

The buzz of my phone stops her. She watches me pick it up from the edge of my chair. Truman's name flashes on my screen. What the heck? He's in Vegas; Ryle's with his parents. Why would he be calling me? If it were about Ryle, it would be one of his parents calling.

I hold my breath as I tap the screen. I've never told Dani that seeing Truman's name flash on my phone screen still gives me butterflies. Just the same way it always did.

"Hey."

"Jules."

He uses my nickname. I used to love it when he called me Jules, especially when he was kissing me. And then I hated it after we split up. He never quit calling me Jules, so I got used to it. Sort of. Still brings to mind things better left in the past.

But right now, he sounds a little panicked.

"What? What's going on?"

"We're at the hospital—"

"What?" I'm out of my chair faster than bikes out of the starting gate in a motocross. "What's going on? Is Ryle okay? What happ—"

"Jules."

I hear Truman take a breath. But his attempt to calm himself only makes my heart pound harder. Dani scrambles off her chair, sensing my rising panic. She gathers my purse and my keys as I slide my bare feet into my sandals.

"What's going on?" she says quietly as I take my keys from her. "Let me drive you."

"Jules, it's not Ryle." Truman's voice is firm, but he still sounds worried. *Oh no.* What if it's Anthony or Lillian? What if his dad had a heart attack? What if— "It's Harper."

"Harper?" I yelp. "What happened to Harper?"

Dani's still watching me, but she takes a step back now. I'm not close with Truman's family, but I like them. I care about them; and the thought of something happening to any of them makes me sick.

But now that I know Ryle is okay, my adrenaline rush has piqued, and I'll crash from the let down soon.

"She had an accident. I just wanted—"

"I'm on my way," I tell him. I lean toward Dani to kiss her cheek and then throw a quick wave at Eric.

"You sure? You want me to drive?" Dani whispers.

"I'm okay."

"Let me know," she says with a nod at my phone still pressed to my ear.

"Thanks." I nod as I turn and hurry to my car. Even knowing that Ryle's okay, I desperately need to get to the hospital and see for myself. I need to put my arms around my son and hold him.

And I need to make sure Harper's okay.

In a perfect world, she would be my sister-in-law.

***

To read more of Truman and Julie's story, click here:

Rings on Wings

ALSO BY TRACY BROEMMER

Four Letter Words, Lorelei Bluffs, Book 6

See Kate, Lorelei Bluffs, Book 7

Loved You More, Lorelei Bluffs, Book 8

A Lorelei Ending, Lorelei Bluffs, Book 9

I Do, Lorelei Bluffs, Book 10

Truth Is, The Williams Legacy, Book 1

Other People's Ugly, The Williams Legacy, Book 2

Omissions, The Williams Legacy, Book 3

Contemporary Romance Novels:

Destiny's Calling: Your Future Is Waiting

Wedding Day Shenanigans

Holiday Fling

The Kiss Off

Something Like Love

Plus One

Hold Onto the Stars, Book #5 in Blue Collar Romance series

The Jane Thing, Book #2 in Meet Cute Book Club series

Shameless Santa, Book #7 in Welcome to Kissing Springs series

Sunshine & Soulmates, Welcome to Kissing Springs, Sunshine Season

Bourbon & Bedposts, Book #7 in Welcome to Kissing Springs, Bourbon Season

Doctor Divine, Doctors of Eastport General, Season 2

Beach Daze, Flamingo Island

Moonlight in Montreal, The Vagabond Series

Christmas and Other Inconveniences, Betting on Christmas Collection

Eggnog in Amesbury, Christmas in Amesbury Series (Sweet Romance)

A December Wish, Wishing for Love Series (Sweet Romance)

A Naughty Lesson

Love, Nashville, The Mississippi Queen Trilogy, Book 1

Forever, Duncan, The Mississippi Queen Trilogy, Book 2

Always, Jess, The Mississippi Queen Trilogy, Book 3

Gettin' Hitched, The H Books, Book 1

Hookin' Up, The H Books, Book 2

Holdin' On, The H Books, Book 2.5

Intoxicate Me, 515 Whiskey, Book .5

Taste Me, 515 Whiskey, Book 1

Scrooge Me, 515 Whiskey, Bonus Short Story in Let's Get Naughty V 3

Contemporary Romance Novellas:

Indian Summer

Dear Jaclyn Perris

French Stuff

Holdin' On (The H Books)

End in Flames

Mistletoe Mishaps

Toasted: A New Year's Eve Novella

Endless Summer (Timberton Hounds)

Homeless Holiday (Timberton Hounds)

Restless Hearts (Timberton Hounds)

Timberton Hounds Novellas Boxset

Boone's Girl

Intoxicate Me (515 Whiskey)

Seducing You (Welcome to Kissing Springs and Lockland Distilling: Keys to Love)

Kissing You (Welcome to Kissing Springs and Lockland Distilling: Keys to Love)

Swipe for Fangs

Swipe for Ghouls

Feels on Wheels (Love in Motion Duet, Book 1) (Sweet Romance)

Rings on Wings (Love in Motion Duet, Book 2) (Sweet Romance)

Love in Motion Boxset

Other Novellas:

The Devy Man, A Horror Novella

Today, Again (Sweet Love Story)

Women's Fiction Short Stories:

India Falls

Luther's Cross: 87,600

The Candy Cane Tree of Willow Lane

Delays

Same Time Next Year

Contemporary Romance Short Stories:

Perfect Pictures, The Wine Tasting Series, Traminette (Sweet)

Coming Home, The Wine Tasting Series, Edelweiss (Sweet)

Save Me Every Dance, The Wine Tasting Series, Rosé (Sweet)

Marry Me, The Wine Tasting Series, Shiraz (Sweet)

Birthday Wishes, The Wine Tasting Series, Muscat (Sweet)

Dad Jeans, The Wine Tasting Series, Vignoles (Sweet)

The Wine Tasting Series Boxset (Sweet)

Peppermint Lane

Priceless Memory (Timberton Hounds)

Truly Dante, A Mississippi Queen Trilogy Short Story

Strawberry Wine

Love Letter

Leaving You, A Lockland Distilling: Keys to Love Short Story

Sambuca Santa

Deadman's Hollow

ABOUT THE AUTHOR

Tracy Broemmer is the author of several contemporary romance novels including the 515 Whiskey Series, the Welcome to Kissing Springs: Bourbon Fever Collection, and the Mississippi Queen Trilogy. Tracy also writes women's fiction and is the author of the Williams Legacy series as well as several stand-alone titles.

Tracy's books have been called gripping, emotional, and timely, and readers describe her characters as real and relatable.

Tracy lives in Midwestern Illinois with her husband of 31 years. Visit her on the web and sign up for her newsletter at www.broemmerbooks.com